Read Between the Crimes

Lucy Averill

AnniesFiction.com

Books in the Secrets of the Castleton Manor Library series

A Novel Murder
Bitter Words
The Grim Reader
A Deadly Chapter
An Autographed Mystery
Second Edition Death
A Crime Well Versed
A Murder Unscripted
Pride and Publishing
A Literary Offense
Up to Noir Good
For Letter or Worse
On Pens and Needles
Ink or Swim
Tell No Tales
Page Fright
A Fatal Yarn
Read Between the Crimes
From Fable to Grave
A Fateful Sentence
Cloak and Grammar
A Lost Clause
A Thorny Plot
A Scary Tale Wedding

Read Between the Crimes
Copyright © 2018, 2023 Annie's.

All rights reserved. No part of this publication may be reproduced, stored in a retrieval system, or transmitted in any form or by any means—electronic, mechanical, photocopying, recording or otherwise—without the prior written permission of the publisher. The only exception is brief quotations in printed reviews. For information address Annie's, 306 East Parr Road, Berne, Indiana 46711-1138.

The characters and events in this book are fictional, and any resemblance to actual persons or events is coincidental.

Library of Congress-in-Publication Data
Read Between the Crimes / by Lucy Averill
p. cm.
ISBN: 978-1-64025-243-1
I. Title
2018952250

AnniesFiction.com
(800) 282-6643
Secrets of the Castleton Manor Library™
Series Creator: Shari Lohner
Series Editor: Lorie Jones
Cover Illustrator: Jesse Reisch

10 11 12 13 14 | Printed in China | 9 8 7 6

1

Faith Newberry gently closed *Little Women* and let out a satisfied sigh. There was nothing like revisiting cherished books from one's childhood to create feelings of nostalgia and contentment. She counted herself fortunate to have spent much of the past few days immersed in Louisa May Alcott's work.

One of the best things about working as the librarian at Castleton Manor in Lighthouse Bay, Massachusetts, was the unfettered access to such an outstanding collection of reading material.

Not only had she spent many pleasurable hours in the familiar company of the famous March sisters, but she had read several short story collections as well as a rarer book written by A. M. Barnard, which was one of Louisa May's pen names.

The ticking of the clock broke the spell. Even though she had awakened early, it was almost time to head to work. Castleton Manor was far more than a sprawling estate with a world-class library. It was an extraordinary venue for all manner of literary events.

A group called the Pickwick Club was arriving for their first Louisa May Alcott conference. Since Faith was an enthusiastic fan of Alcott's work, she was already caught up in the excitement.

Truth be told, Faith loved all the literary events hosted by the manor. She still couldn't believe she had been fortunate enough to be hired for such a unique position.

As much as Faith was certain the members of the Pickwick Club would approve of her recent choices in reading material, she was also certain they would appreciate it if she opened the library on time. She reminded herself that her comfy reading spot would still be there when she returned home in the evening.

She stood and put her coat on, then plucked a wool lace shawl from the back of the sofa and wrapped it around her shoulders. The quaint old gardener's cottage was warm and cozy thanks to the crackling fire in the fireplace, but the air outside was still brisk this time of year in New England. March might be spring according to the calendar, but it rarely felt like it to Faith.

"Are you planning to join me, Watson?" she asked her black-and-white tuxedo cat, who was lounging on the sofa. "Or would you rather stay here for a catnap?"

Watson blinked twice, then stretched luxuriantly before jumping down and dashing ahead of her to the cottage door.

She smiled. "I guess you're coming." She crossed the gleaming hardwood floor to the door.

Faith made her way across the lawn with Watson close at her side. The grass was damp, and every few steps he stopped to shake the dew from his paws.

She bent down and scooped him up, then tucked him under the warmth of her shawl. "Is that better?" she asked.

The cat pressed his face against her neck and purred.

Faith hurried past the topiaries and rosebushes that separated her home from the manor, then entered the opulent building.

The sound of excited chatter grew louder as she made her way along the Great Hall Gallery.

Faith spotted a tall, powerfully built woman holding a Chinese crested dog under her arm. The dog and the woman wore matching green cable-knit sweaters.

The tiny dog began to bark furiously at Watson.

"Rapunzel, stop that right now," the woman said. She smiled at Faith and extended a hand. "I'm Deb Fremont, one of the members of the Pickwick Club. I don't believe we've met."

She grasped the woman's hand and gave it a firm shake. "Faith Newberry, the librarian here at Castleton Manor, and this is Watson.

I'm delighted to meet you and Rapunzel."

The quivering dog growled and tried to lunge at Watson.

"I'm so sorry," Deb said. "I can't imagine what's gotten into Rapunzel. She usually loves cats as much as I do." She held out the back of her hand to Watson for him to inspect.

Faith appreciated the other woman's understanding of Watson's personal space. Some of the guests at the manor were overeager in their interactions with her cat. They all seemed to mean well, but that didn't always make it easy for Watson to endure the extra attention.

Watson leaned toward Deb and gave her hand a delicate sniff. He glanced at Faith as if to say that she met with his approval.

Rapunzel seemed even more upset by Watson's presence once it was clear that the cat and her mistress were likely to get along.

Ever the accommodating host, Watson took his leave. He squirmed in Faith's arms, and when she let him down, he shot off down the hallway.

"If I had known you were going to be so unsociable, I would have left you in a tower somewhere, young lady," Deb chided her dog. She smiled apologetically at Faith. "I hope Watson won't hold her rudeness against her."

"He understands, and I expect that's why he ran off," Faith said. "I'm sure the two of you will enjoy the conference once Rapunzel gets comfortable. Pets always seem to have as much fun as their owners at the manor."

"I certainly hope so," Deb said, then checked her watch. "Oh my, we've got to dash. One of the sessions is about to start." She gave Faith a bright smile and hurried down the hall.

The cat trotted down the corridor, attempting to put as much distance as he could between him and the unpleasant canine he'd just met.

There were many other unfamiliar creatures in the manor today. It must be the beginning of one of those events his human helped with. Generally, he made it a practice to avoid dogs even if their owners were pleasant sorts of people. It was a rule that had served him well, and he had no intention of bending it this week.

Still, he needed to make the rounds and evaluate the newcomers. Even though none of them would be staying for too long, he preferred to know exactly who had entered his territory. After all, he had his human to protect.

The animal visitors were of interest to him, of course, but their human companions were at least as important to investigate. His own human was more likely to interact with them. He didn't think she was a bad judge of character, but she tended to see the good in all creatures. He was much more apprehensive and considered it his duty to be vigilant on her behalf.

His whiskers twitched. Another canine was arriving.

The cat proceeded down the hall and stopped in his tracks when he spotted a little white dog contentedly tripping along next to her master. The cat didn't understand how dogs seemed to enjoy being on leashes. It was so undignified.

The dog grinned at him.

He huffed in derision and turned away.

Faith took the stairs to the basement level and followed the scent of cinnamon to the kitchen.

Brooke Milner, the head chef and her good friend, glanced up from the counter where she was working when Faith appeared in the doorway.

Without a word, Brooke reached into a cupboard and pulled out a delicate china teacup. She deftly filled it with hot water from a kettle on the stove, dropped in a tea bag, and held it out to Faith. "You look like you need this," she said with a twinkle in her blue eyes.

"Thank you." Faith held the cup beneath her chilly nose and inhaled the fragrant steam. "Just the thing to start the workday," she said after taking a sip.

"Can I tempt you with one or two of these?" Brooke asked, holding out a large platter piled with scones, muffins, turnovers, and cinnamon rolls.

Faith smiled. "How could I resist?" She chose a cinnamon roll and set it on a small plate. Then she carried her plate and teacup to the table in the back corner of the kitchen and took a seat.

Brooke handed her an ornate silver fork and a crisp white napkin and sat down across from her.

Faith took a bite of the roll. "It's delicious. I'll never open the library on time at this rate."

"Maybe I should give you a doggie bag," Brooke said with a grin.

"Watson prefers to call them kitty bags." Faith took another bite and thought for the thousandth time how lucky she was to be able to sample Brooke's culinary delights day in and day out.

"Oh, I almost forgot," Brooke said. "Wolfe was in here a few moments ago searching for you. He said he'll meet you in the library."

"Did he say why?" Faith asked. Wolfe Jaxon was the handsome co-owner of Castleton Manor and Faith's boss.

"He wants to talk to you about the unveiling ceremony."

Faith swallowed quickly, slid her plate with the half-eaten roll across the table to her friend, and jumped up. "I've got to scoot."

"Just a second." Brooke got up and popped the rest of the cinnamon roll, a turnover, and a muffin into a paper bag and folded down the top. She also filled a travel mug with tea. "Now you'll be all set until lunchtime."

"Thanks. What would I do without you?" Faith grabbed the mug and the bag, then rushed out the door and upstairs.

Faith spotted Wolfe standing in the Great Hall Gallery. She quickened her pace to catch up with him.

"No need to rush," Wolfe said. "I wanted to be sure to catch you. I thought we could talk on your way to the library."

"That would be great," Faith said with relief. "Brooke said you wanted to check in with me about something involving the unveiling ceremony." She felt the tiniest flutter in her chest as she met his striking blue gaze.

"That's right," Wolfe said. "I wanted to see if *The Maiden's Plight* is ready for its debut."

Several months earlier, the news had broken that *The Maiden's Plight* and *The Damsel's Fate*—a two-volume blood-and-thunder novel—had actually been written by Louisa May Alcott under a previously unknown pen name. Alcott had written many works of fiction under pen names, but not all of them had been attributed to her during her lifetime.

When word had spread through the book world about the discovery, Faith and Wolfe had been thrilled to discover that the manor's collection contained *The Maiden's Plight*, the first book of the two-volume novel. Faith was even more excited to realize that the rare book was in exceptional condition. She had sent the volume out for appraisal immediately, and she had not felt entirely comfortable until it had been returned to the locked case in the library.

"I have the book stored in one of the cases under lock and key," Faith said. "Laura has polished the glass so much that I think she may wear a hole in it." She smiled at the enthusiasm Laura Kettrick brought to her duties at the manor. Laura mainly worked in housekeeping, but sometimes she assisted Faith in the library.

"I'm looking forward to the presentation this evening when the book is reunited with its sequel," Wolfe said. His voice always took on a note of pleasure when discussing the cherished items in the manor's library collection.

Faith shared his delight completely. "I still can't believe Ms. Langston brought it with her to the conference."

The keynote speaker for the event, Vanessa Langston, had graciously offered to bring her copy of *The Damsel's Fate* to the manor in order for the two books to be displayed together. The opportunity to see the rare books on display was one of the many reasons the Pickwick Club had decided to hold its conference at Castleton. Faith also knew that Wolfe was planning to see if Vanessa would sell him the volume for the manor's collection.

Vanessa was an internationally best-selling and beloved novelist. She had made a name for herself by writing at least a dozen historical novels, and she had recently announced her contract to write the Littlest Women series, a continuation of Louisa May Alcott's Little Women series.

Faith was not entirely sure she approved of another author taking over where Alcott had left off, but she would keep that opinion to herself while Vanessa was a guest at the manor. She assumed there were other Alcott fans who shared her opinion, but she didn't wish to dampen anyone else's enthusiasm.

"I'm sure Ms. Langston is just as excited as we are to see the two volumes together in one place," Wolfe said.

"With her particular interest in Louisa May Alcott's work, I assume she is," Faith replied.

"I intend to pick up the book from the library sometime before the panel this afternoon, so don't be alarmed if you don't see it in the case," Wolfe said. "I wouldn't want you to worry that it had gone missing."

"Please don't even joke about it," Faith said. "I don't know what I'd do if anything happened to the books in the collection, but I'd be beside myself over *The Maiden's Plight*."

"Then I'll make a point to resist any further teasing on that subject." Wolfe smiled. "I have complete confidence that you have the security completely in hand."

"Thank you," Faith said. Wolfe was a wonderful employer, and she was always happy to hear he was satisfied with her work.

When they arrived at the library door, Wolfe stopped and faced her. "While we're on the subject of Alcott, I wanted to ask your opinion on another matter."

"Of course. What can I do for you?"

"In honor of our current guests, I've been inspired to reread *Little Women*."

"I just reread it too," Faith said with a smile.

"Good, so it's fresh in your mind as well," Wolfe said. "I was curious about your opinion of the gentlemen. Do you think Jo made the right decision in marrying Professor Bhaer? Or should she have accepted Laurie's offer?"

"I think Jo chose wisely," Faith answered. "I always felt that Laurie was a bit too frivolous for her, with his enjoyment of parties and the finer things in life. She was always happiest alone with a book and an apple. And I think their short tempers would have made for a tumultuous marriage at best. I like the professor for her because he challenged her to be a better, calmer, and more thoughtful person." She stopped and flushed. She frequently got carried away when talking about her beloved literature. "But perhaps you should ask one of the Alcott scholars."

"They may be experts, but yours is the opinion I most value." With that, Wolfe nodded and walked away.

Beaming over the compliment, Faith unlocked the door and stepped inside the library.

Every time she entered the room, her breath caught in her throat, and today was no different. The room was too beautiful to be taken for granted. Even without the valuable collection of first editions, it would have impressed visitors. From the soaring bookcases lining every wall to the immense fireplace and plush wingback chairs, the room was built to entrance booklovers.

As soon as she crossed the threshold, Watson appeared out of nowhere, as he so often did, and rubbed against her ankles.

"What have you been up to, Rumpy?" she asked, calling him by his nickname. She'd given it to him because he'd lost most of his tail in an accident when he was a kitten.

Watson, who didn't appreciate the undignified moniker one bit, huffed and sauntered over to the fireplace. He jumped onto the settee and curled up.

She wished she could join him, but between the conference and the unveiling ceremony, her to-do list was longer than usual. Even with assistance from Laura, there was always a great deal to do to keep the library running smoothly.

Faith's duties included far more than opening the library and providing guests with books on a wide range of topics. In addition, she sent books out for repair and sought out new volumes to add to the collection. She kept up on the value of rare volumes and had them appraised for insurance purposes. Of course, she also shelved books and responded to e-mails from other libraries all over the world that wrote with questions about the Castleton Manor collection.

Despite the busyness, she loved her job, and she would not have had it any other way. Wolfe provided a generous budget, and she prided herself on making good investments on behalf of the library and in seeing the value of the collection grow. It was deeply rewarding.

Faith took a seat behind her ornately carved desk and pulled out a notebook. As she went over her to-do list, she was relieved that she had no scheduled obligations with the conference this morning. She might be able to get through her tasks by lunchtime.

"Excuse me," a warm, friendly voice called across the large room. "Are you the librarian?"

Faith glanced up and saw a petite, russet-haired woman standing in the doorway. "I am indeed. How may I help you?" she asked.

The woman made her way to Faith's desk, a huge tote bag slung over her shoulder. Faith marveled at how the diminutive woman could carry such a large burden.

"I'm Theresa Collins, the president of the Pickwick Club. Ms. Russell said you could help me with our newsletter." She held out her hand.

As she shook it, Faith kept her smile firmly in place and hoped she hadn't actually groaned out loud. Marlene Russell was the manor's prickly yet extremely efficient assistant manager and Faith's supervisor, so it seemed like her plans to cross everything off her to-do list by lunch had just gone out the window.

"What sort of help did you have in mind?" Faith asked.

"I want to produce a special edition of our group's newsletter," Theresa said. "Usually we send out an e-mail newsletter that covers club meetings and member news and the field trips we're planning."

"How do you intend to make this one special?" Faith asked, gesturing at the seat across from her.

Theresa sat down and placed her enormous bag on her lap. "I'd like to create one that sounds like it was written by the March sisters," she answered, her voice brimming with enthusiasm. "Are you familiar with the *Pickwick Portfolio*?"

"I believe that's the name Jo and her sisters gave to the newspaper they wrote," Faith replied, glad she had taken the time to reread *Little Women*.

"Exactly," Theresa said. "I want to create our own version to hand out to the attendees as a souvenir of their time at Castleton Manor."

"I think it's a charming idea," Faith said. "But I'm not sure how I can be of assistance. I'm not very familiar with your club."

"For this edition, I want to skip all the usual articles and focus on things that girls like Meg and Jo would have been interested in writing about during the Civil War. That's why Ms. Russell suggested I contact you."

"Are you looking for resources here in the library?"

"Absolutely. But Ms. Russell said you could also help me write the articles," Theresa replied. "I'm more of a reader than a writer, but I really want this newsletter to be something the members of the Pickwick Club will treasure as a keepsake from this event."

Faith leaned back in her chair and considered the request. She had very little expertise in crafting newsletters, but she was intrigued by the idea of creating something inspired by one of her favorite books. It could prove to be an enormous amount of fun to write the newsletter as if she were one of the characters. She could feel her worries over the rest of her tasks fading away as the idea took hold in her mind.

"When do you want to start?" Faith asked.

Theresa patted her tote bag and smiled. "Since I've brought most of my collection of Alcott's works as well as some notes, how about right now?"

Faith raised her arms above her head and stretched. She and Theresa had been camped out at the table in the library for over an hour, working on ideas for the newsletter.

Theresa had brought half a dozen notebooks, stacks of newspaper clippings, and volumes of Alcott's work as source material for the newsletter project. Even though Faith had not been pleased to hear that Marlene had volunteered her to help without consulting her, she had to admit the project was clever as well as enjoyable.

A couple of patrons entered the library, and Faith went over to greet them.

After showing them the collection of Louisa May Alcott books, Faith returned to the table. She was surprised to see Theresa gathering her things and stuffing them back into her bag. "Is something wrong?" Faith asked.

Theresa snorted. "This library may be large, but I don't believe there's room enough in it for both Vanessa Langston and me."

Faith turned to see an attractive blonde making her way toward the table where they were working. The woman wore black dress pants and a pale-blue silk blouse.

"If I have to speak to Vanessa again today, I'm not sure I can be responsible for my actions," Theresa muttered. "Will you be able to help me again later?"

"Just stop by the library anytime," Faith replied.

"Thank you," Theresa said, then bolted from the room.

"So this is the library everyone keeps praising," Vanessa stated as she approached the table. She wrinkled her nose as she gazed around the room. "I suppose it's adequate."

Faith stifled a gasp. She couldn't imagine anyone describing anything about Castleton Manor as merely adequate, least of all the library. Then she reminded herself that she was hired to serve all the guests, even the ones she didn't agree with.

She pasted on a smile. "I'm Faith Newberry, the librarian here. How may I help you?"

"I'd like to take a peek at the library's copy of *The Maiden's Plight*," Vanessa said. "I want to see it for myself before the masses clamor around, especially if they're anything like Tiresome Theresa."

The insult rankled Faith, who had enjoyed Theresa's company, but she had to maintain a professional attitude. "Of course. Please follow me." She led the way to an alcove positioned at the far side of the library, where a display case sat sheltered from any harmful rays of sunlight that filtered into the room. Even in the soft light, the excellent condition of *The Maiden's Plight* was plain to see.

"Aren't you going to pull it out and let me take a good look at it?" Vanessa tapped the glass, leaving fingerprints on the gleaming surface.

At least now Laura will have a real reason to pull out her cleaning cloth again, Faith thought. "I'd be happy to. Just let me fetch the key and some gloves."

Vanessa folded her arms across her chest. "Why did you lock it up?"

"It's simply a routine safety precaution we use for extremely rare volumes," Faith said, trying to keep her tone light and friendly. She was surprised that a rare-book owner would need to be convinced of the necessity of such care.

"Well, I don't intend to go to any unnecessary fuss," Vanessa huffed.

"If you'd like, we can place your volume in the manor's safe," Faith said.

Vanessa waved a hand in front of her. "I prefer to have easy access to it. I'm using it as research material for my Littlest Women series."

Once again, Faith was surprised at Vanessa's nonchalant attitude toward such a precious volume.

"Do you have any lesser-known biographies, correspondence, or newspaper articles referencing Louisa May Alcott in your collection?" Vanessa asked.

"We might. I'll have to check," Faith said. "And perhaps you could ask at Orchard House during the trip planned later in the week."

Orchard House was the historic home of the Alcott family, and it was where Louisa May Alcott wrote and set *Little Women*. Faith was sure the tour of the house would be one of the highlights of the conference for the attendees.

"I'm already spending too much of my valuable time attending this event," Vanessa snapped. "I insist you check to see if you have what I'm asking for."

"I'll look here and also at the Candle House Library," Faith said. Her aunt, Eileen Piper, was the head librarian there. If anyone could help, it would be her. "They may have some additional resources, or they might be able to offer some other suggestions."

"I suppose that will have to do," Vanessa said. She turned her back on Faith as if to dismiss her and headed to a chair positioned next to the giant stone fireplace, where flames flickered in the grate.

Faith watched as Vanessa pulled a cell phone from her pocket and unlocked the screen, bathing her pale face in electronic light. It seemed that although Vanessa was too busy to do her own research, she had enough time to check her social media.

Faith focused her own attention on the card catalog.

But before she could even finish entering the name *Louisa May Alcott* into the search bar, she heard a shriek.

2

Startled, Faith rushed to the source of the scream.

Watson sat calmly on Vanessa's lap. He held one sleek white paw aloft and cleaned it thoroughly, paying no mind whatsoever to the distress he was causing the author.

"Get it off!" Vanessa squealed. "Get it off me right now!" She held her hands in front of her face as though shielding herself from a physical blow.

"I'm so sorry he upset you," Faith said, lifting Watson from Vanessa's lap.

The other woman shot up from the chair and took several steps away from the cat.

"There's nothing to be afraid of," Faith assured her. "Watson would never hurt anyone."

Watson jumped down and stood at Faith's feet. His ears flattened against his head as he stared at Vanessa. If Faith had to guess, she would have said he was offended. She could hardly blame him.

"I absolutely despise cats," Vanessa declared. She glanced down at her outfit and frowned. "That animal has left fur all over me. Now I need to go and change." She hurried out the door without a backward glance.

"I suppose I should be cross with you," Faith said, bending down to pat Watson on the head. His ears pricked back up as she rubbed them. "But you've done me an enormous favor by sending her on her way. I'm not sure I could have held my tongue if we'd spent any more time together. Now I understand why Theresa was in such a hurry to get away from her."

Watson bumped her leg with his nose and stared up at Faith as if to say, "You're welcome." Then he returned to his seat in front of the fireplace.

Faith decided to skip lunch, even though the smells wafting down the hall from the dining room tempted her to join the happy throng of guests. The steady stream of library patrons had not let up after Vanessa fled the library, and this was her first opportunity to head for the Candle House Library in downtown Lighthouse Bay. Faith always felt it best to get things done as quickly as possible, especially if she had made a commitment to someone else.

She picked up her shawl and draped it loosely across her shoulders. She needed to hurry if she wanted to conduct the research for Vanessa and get back to the manor in time to attend an afternoon panel discussion.

There was almost no traffic to speak of, and in no time at all she was parking at the Candle House Library. As she entered the building, sunlight filtered in through the original glass carefully preserved in the windows.

The library was housed in the historic stone building formerly used to manufacture candles, hence its name. The conversion from an unused workspace into a thriving library had been executed with both sensitivity and care. Everywhere Faith looked, signs of the building's past were on display. She loved being in this library almost as much as she loved being in the one at the manor.

Aunt Eileen rushed over and gave her a warm hug. "What brings you by? I thought you'd have your hands full with the Alcott conference this week."

"Actually I'm here on behalf of the conference," Faith said.

"I'm intrigued. Come on back." Eileen led the way to her office, then gestured to the small table tucked into a corner.

Faith took a seat and smiled. "I'm here on an errand for a certain writer I believe you're familiar with."

Eileen sat down across from her. "You don't mean Vanessa Langston, do you?" She leaned forward, her blue eyes twinkling.

Faith nodded. "She came by this morning and asked for Louisa May Alcott biographies and primary source materials. I told her I'd find out if you had any here."

"We have quite a few resources that will help Vanessa," Eileen said. "But Bernadette Varney is using them right now."

"The author of *The Winds of Fortune*?" Faith asked. Several months ago, she and the other members of the Candle House Book Club had read the swashbuckling tale of adventure and romance. Faith had enjoyed it so much that she immediately read the sequel.

Eileen nodded. "She came in about an hour ago asking for materials and a space to work. It was a surprise to see her in town."

"One of the panelists at the convention had to cancel, and Bernadette agreed to fill in at the last minute," Faith explained.

"And you didn't tell me?" Eileen asked in mock horror.

Faith held up her hands. "I just found out about it. Marlene stopped by the library to tell me right before I left to come here."

"Let's go see how Bernadette's doing," Eileen suggested. "Maybe she's done with the materials by now. Or maybe she could use some help putting together a presentation on such short notice."

Faith followed her aunt into the main section of the library.

A woman in her late twenties sat at a long table in the center of the room. All around her lay open books and file folders. Her head was bent over a laptop, and her fingers flew across the keys.

Eileen approached Bernadette at the table. "I'm sorry to bother you, but I'd like you to meet my niece Faith Newberry. She's the librarian at Castleton Manor."

Bernadette glanced up. She had a generous smattering of freckles on her nose and cheeks. "Oh, it's nice to meet you." Her voice was soft but friendly.

Faith had to lean forward slightly to hear her. "You too. I

understand you're filling in for one of the panelists at the convention this afternoon."

Bernadette nodded. "I did my thesis on some of Louisa May Alcott's work, and Dr. Johnson, my adviser from the university, suggested me as a replacement."

"How exciting," Eileen said.

"Public speaking is not my favorite thing," Bernadette admitted. "But Dr. Johnson convinced me it was a smart career move, so I agreed. This experience will be impressive on my résumé."

"I'm looking forward to attending the panel," Faith said. "And by the way, I love your books."

Bernadette blushed. "That's very kind of you to say."

Faith had a hard time reconciling the shy and retiring young woman she saw in front of her with the author of *The Winds of Fortune*. Somehow she had pictured that such a story would have sprung from the imagination of a far more flamboyant individual.

"You're definitely an up-and-coming historical novelist," Eileen chimed in.

"I'm not sure I would go so far as to say that," Bernadette murmured. "I've had a few books published—that's all." She gently closed the lid on her laptop and stared down at it.

"I'd say a few published books is quite an accomplishment," Faith commented. "Most people don't publish any."

Bernadette seemed even more uncomfortable at the praise. She shrugged and continued to stare at the closed computer in front of her.

"It's not just the number of books," Eileen said. "It's the quality of them. I recommend them to all our patrons who express interest in historical fiction." She placed a hand on Bernadette's shoulder. "I can honestly tell you that every time patrons return your books, they never fail to ask if you've written any others. I can't keep them on the shelves."

"Thank you," Bernadette said. "That's so nice to hear."

"How are you doing with the Alcott resources?" Eileen asked. "Have they been useful?"

"Yes, they were exactly what I needed to jump-start my work in progress." Bernadette began closing the books and folders. "I'm done with them."

"Are you sure you're finished?" Faith asked. "I need to borrow them, but I don't want to rush you."

"You're not rushing me," Bernadette assured her. She slid the reference books across the table.

"Thank you." Faith collected the books and dropped them into her bag.

Bernadette checked her watch. "I need to call a taxi to take me back to the manor. I don't want to be late for the panel discussion."

"Would you like a ride?" Faith said. "My car's right outside."

"Are you sure it's not too much trouble?" Bernadette stood and gathered her laptop, notebook, and folders, then put them into her canvas backpack.

"I have all that I came for," Faith said, patting her bag. "And I'm going to the manor anyway." She suddenly had an idea. Maybe Bernadette would be willing to assist them with the Pickwick Club's newsletter. "Also, I'm wondering if you can help me out with something."

"I'm not sure if I can, but I'll certainly try," Bernadette said. She hoisted the backpack onto her shoulders.

Faith hugged her aunt. "Thanks for everything. I'll talk to you later."

"Anytime," Eileen said, then waved them out the door.

On the way to the car, Faith explained what was on her mind. "Theresa Collins asked me to help create a newsletter as a souvenir of the conference. She wants to craft articles for it that sound as though they were written by the March sisters. Would you mind taking a peek at what we've got so far?"

Bernadette grinned, revealing two faint dimples, one in each cheek. "What a great idea. I'd love to check it out."

"Wonderful," Faith said as she grasped the door handle of her car and slid into the driver's seat. "When are you free to discuss it?"

"I can stop by the library after the panel." Bernadette smiled. "It'll give me something to take my mind off speaking in front of a large audience."

"That sounds perfect. Now let's get you back to the manor before my boss sends out a search party." Faith didn't want to consider what Marlene would have to say if she caused any delays in the schedule.

For the rest of the ride, Bernadette was silent. She gazed out the window, fiddling with the strap on her backpack.

She must be really nervous about her speech. Faith couldn't blame her. She'd given several presentations during her time at Castleton Manor, and she didn't think she'd ever get used to public speaking.

When they arrived at the manor, Faith had barely stopped the car before Bernadette thanked her, hopped out, and dashed off.

Faith followed at a slightly more sedate pace. She wanted to attend the panel, but as a member of staff she wanted to be sure all the best seats were available for the guests. By the time she arrived in the music room, it was standing room only.

Faith found a spot near a pink-cheeked man wearing an electric-blue sweater vest covered in long white silky hairs. She wondered if they had come from a dog or a cat. She smiled at him. "Welcome to Castleton. I'm Faith Newberry, the librarian here."

He shook her hand. "Good to meet you. I'm Marcus Tripp, Vanessa Langston's literary agent."

Before they could continue the conversation, Theresa appeared at the lectern at the front of the room and tapped on the microphone.

The audience quieted down.

"Good afternoon, everyone." Theresa beamed at the assembled crowd. "I always knew I was not alone in my love of *Little Women*, but it is very gratifying to see the proof with my own eyes. Please join me in welcoming our esteemed panel of experts."

The audience applauded.

A striking woman with closely cropped curly hair and warm brown skin mounted the steps to the panelists' table and took a seat behind the name placard *Dr. Beverly Johnson*.

Bernadette followed her onto the stage, tripping on the last step and nearly losing her balance completely.

Faith felt her heart go out to the nervous young woman and sent up a silent word of prayer that she would find a way to enjoy the experience.

After a pause, Vanessa Langston appeared. She had swapped her earlier outfit for a dramatic asymmetrical black dress that most women would have considered too formal for day wear. Vanessa glided up the stairs, leaving little question as to which panelist felt most comfortable in the spotlight. She took her seat and smiled at the audience.

Faith had to admit that the author knew how to make a grand entrance.

Vanessa leaned toward her microphone. "Before we begin, I'd like to remind you that this evening our host, Wolfe Jaxon, and I are presenting a joint unveiling of our volumes *The Maiden's Plight* and *The Damsel's Fate* in the Great Hall Gallery."

There was a burst of applause from the crowd.

"I know we're all looking forward to it," Theresa said. She sat down at the head of the table, where she would act as moderator. "Now let's meet our esteemed panelists." She introduced the women, then glanced down at the note cards in her hand. "I'd like to start by asking each of you why you feel Louisa May Alcott's work has had such a lasting impact."

Faith's attention drifted away from the panelists, and she gazed around the room. Often guests at the manor would dress up in honor of their favorite author or character. She recalled rabid enthusiasts of Sherlock Holmes wearing deerstalker caps and capes. But the attendees of this convention were mostly women of all ages wearing a wide variety of outfits.

For this convention, Faith would have expected a lot of gowns from the Civil War era, but going by the clothing here, she would not have been able to guess which author these women were celebrating. Perhaps that was the enduring legacy of Louisa May Alcott. The author still maintained a broad appeal to many different kinds of women, and her work meant something special to each of them. Clearly, these fans had all chosen to pay tribute to her in their own ways.

Across the room, she noticed a young woman with short dark hair and black thick-rimmed glasses. She appeared uninterested in the discussion as she typed on her laptop. Faith thought she was being rather rude, but maybe she was taking notes on the discussion.

Faith's attention snapped back to the panelists' table when she heard heated voices.

"Alcott's work was groundbreaking on so many levels," Beverly said sharply. "It's disheartening to think that she is most remembered for churning out what she herself called 'moral pap for the young.'"

"It seems to me that she realized that much of her work would do her no credit," Vanessa retorted. "*Little Women* and the other books she wrote for the young were what she wanted associated with her name. She wrote her more scandalous stories under a pen name, which tells me that she was ashamed of them."

"Alcott wrote *Little Women* and her other children's stories to make a living," Beverly said, her voice becoming louder with each word. "She was unhappy and struggled to find her place in a restrictive world. She found no joy in the work." She turned to Bernadette. "Don't you agree?"

For a moment, Bernadette appeared startled at being put on the spot. "While I can't speak for Alcott, we do know from her own letters and journal entries that she found the popularity of her children's books to be surprising. I think it's safe to say that she never expected to earn a fortune from them."

"We also know that she wrote *Little Women* only at the urging of her father, who felt there would be a market for it," Beverly added.

"That was then, and this is now," Vanessa said. "Which is why my new series continuing the Little Women books is so eagerly awaited by the public." She smiled at the audience. "I'm sure you have all preordered a copy of my new book that will be released next year."

A murmur traveled through the crowd.

Faith glanced around the room, watching the guests' reactions. Many attendees nodded eagerly, but just as many leaned back and folded their arms across their chests.

A petite brown-haired woman seated in the center of the room shot to her feet. She raised her arm and gestured wildly.

Theresa nodded at the woman. "Do you have a question?"

"Ms. Langston, how is what you're doing any different than fan fiction?"

Vanessa appeared taken aback, but she quickly regained her composure. "While I'm proud to proclaim myself a rabid fan of Louisa May Alcott's work," she said smoothly, "I take issue with my writing being labeled fan fiction."

"Why is that?" the brunette asked.

Vanessa narrowed her eyes. "Because I'm a professional writer. What I'm doing is not in the same league with those who clumsily dabble in the art of writing and then foist their pathetic efforts onto the public through the Internet."

A rumble rippled through the crowd. Vanessa didn't seem to be making any friends with her scathing criticism.

Faith knew fan fiction was a popular pastime with many readers, and she wondered at the wisdom of behaving so dismissively toward them. Vanessa was most likely alienating some of her fan base.

"So you see no similarity between what you're working on and the stories your devoted readers have created to continue your own work?" the brunette insisted.

Faith was impressed. She wasn't sure she could have asked such a question if Vanessa had been pinning such a formidable glare on her.

Vanessa shook her head. "Not in the least. No matter how enthusiastic the people who compose fan fiction may be, the fact remains that they are not professionals."

"Then why is it that several of your last few novels seem to have been copied directly from fan-fiction forums dedicated to your work?" the woman persisted.

Several people in the audience gasped, including Faith.

"That is an outrageous lie," Vanessa shot back. "Who are you to go around making such an accusation?"

"My name is Carol Lynn Dodge, and I'm one of those fan-fiction writers you seem to disdain. But you're not above stealing ideas from us for your own paid work. The entire concept for the Littlest Women series was mine."

3

A collective gasp went through the crowd.

Faith swung her attention from the commotion at the center of the room to the reaction of the other two panelists at the front. A slight smile played across Beverly's face. Bernadette hunched her shoulders and stared down at the table.

Vanessa arched her eyebrows and shook her head slowly as if she pitied Carol Lynn Dodge. "And that, ladies and gentlemen, is one of the downsides to extreme success in the publishing world. There are no new ideas. Any similarities my novels contain to other works are simply a coincidence. And I can assure you that I do not read fan fiction of my own work." She gave Carol Lynn a cloyingly sweet smile. "Since I'm sure you can't back up your claim, I would appreciate it if you kept your accusations to yourself."

"But I can prove that you stole my ideas," Carol Lynn retorted. "Anyone who is interested in seeing the evidence for themselves can find me after the panel. I'd be happy to show you all what I wrote and when it went online."

Theresa got up from the table, plucked Vanessa's microphone from her hand, and addressed the audience. "That concludes our panel for the afternoon. Thank you for attending. Now please join me in a round of applause for our esteemed guests." She tucked the microphone under her arm and clapped.

As soon as the smattering of applause faded away, the members of the audience filed out of the room. Some bolted as though they couldn't wait to distance themselves from the awkward turn the panel had taken. Others quickly followed Carol Lynn.

Faith went to the front of the room to see if she could be of any assistance.

But before she could talk to Theresa, Vanessa stormed over to the conference organizer. "How did that woman get in here? And why was she allowed to make those absurd claims?"

"I had no idea she would accuse you of anything," Theresa protested. "I'm sorry it happened, but we didn't exactly run background checks on people who signed up for the conference."

Vanessa eyed Theresa suspiciously. "I don't believe you. I think you orchestrated the whole thing. You wanted to embarrass me in front of my readers."

Theresa put a hand over her chest, obviously shocked at the accusation. "I had nothing to do with it. I had no idea Carol Lynn would create a disturbance."

"Don't let anything like this happen again, or you'll regret it," Vanessa threatened, then shoved Theresa as she stormed past her.

The shove seemed to take Theresa by surprise. She tumbled from the stage and landed in a heap on the floor.

As Faith hurried to help Theresa, the young woman with short dark hair and black thick-rimmed glasses rushed past her, grasped Vanessa by the elbow, and swiftly ushered her to the door.

Theresa glared at Vanessa as she left.

Faith knelt next to Theresa. "Are you okay?"

"I think so," Theresa said as Faith offered her an arm and she slowly got to her feet. "Did Vanessa push me deliberately?"

"I'm sure it was an accident," Faith said. "She certainly could not have meant for you to fall off the stage."

Theresa clenched her fists. "I'm not so sure. She accused me of planning Carol Lynn's interruption, but I didn't know anything about it."

"Let's hope she gets over any bad feelings before the unveiling ceremony this evening," Faith said. "I would hate for the focus to be on anything but Louisa May Alcott's work."

"I wouldn't count on it," Theresa muttered. "As much as Vanessa said she was angry about the confrontation, I got the distinct impression she actually enjoyed it."

Faith wanted to say something reassuring, but she had come to the same conclusion.

While she hoped Vanessa's attitude wouldn't spoil the convention, she couldn't help but worry that things might take an even worse turn.

Faith hadn't had the chance to give the Alcott reference materials to Vanessa before the discussion panel, so she retrieved the books from the library and delivered them to the author's suite.

When she knocked on the door of the Louisa May Alcott Suite, it opened, and Vanessa poked her head around it. "Oh, it's you. What do you want?" she asked.

Faith held up the materials she'd brought from the Candle House Library. "I have those source materials you asked for."

Vanessa took them and examined them. "I suppose these will do for a start anyway." Before Faith could say another word, Vanessa shut the door in her face.

Faith tried not to let Vanessa's rudeness bother her as she headed to the library.

After the showdown at the afternoon panel, Faith wasn't sure if Theresa would want to continue working on the newsletter, so she was pleasantly surprised to find her waiting at the library door when she returned. The young woman with short dark hair and glasses who had escorted Vanessa from the discussion was with her.

Theresa smiled, but Faith thought she appeared tired.

The other woman, however, seemed to brim with energy. "You must be Faith," she said, extending a hand. "I'm Meredith Harris."

Faith shook her hand. "Yes I am, and it's nice to meet you."

"When I heard Theresa was planning a special newsletter," Meredith continued, "I volunteered to put in a few hours."

"That's great." Faith unlocked the door and stepped back so Theresa and Meredith could enter the library first. "Actually, it seemed like a lot of work for the two of us, so I asked Bernadette Varney to pitch in too. Is that okay with you, Theresa?"

"Of course. We could use all the help we can get."

Faith led the women over to the large table. "We'll have plenty of room to work here."

Watson walked in and strolled over to them, then jumped onto Faith's lap after she sat down.

"What a handsome cat," Meredith remarked.

Watson closed his eyes and purred.

"He appreciates your good taste," Faith said with a smile.

Theresa removed the materials she and Faith had used that morning from her tote bag and spread them out on the table. "I must admit, I'm happy for the distraction that the newsletter will provide."

"Why do you need a distraction?" Meredith asked as she studied the materials.

"I hadn't realized how much stress the conference would create," Theresa answered, running a hand through her hair. She picked up one of the notebooks and began to flip through it. "It seemed like such a good idea when it was still in the planning stages."

Faith felt her heart go out to Theresa. Even with all the help a professional venue like Castleton Manor could provide, running a conference was a huge responsibility. Difficult personalities like Vanessa's made the task even more challenging.

"I think you've been doing a wonderful job," Faith said. "All conferences encounter a few bumps in the road, but overall I'd say this one is off to a good start."

"I agree," Meredith chimed in. "It seems like everyone in the

Pickwick Club is enjoying themselves enormously."

Theresa glanced up from the notebook and smiled at them. "It's nice of you both to say so. But after what happened on the panel this afternoon, I have my doubts."

"I don't think you'll have to worry about anything like that happening again," Meredith said. "The worst is definitely over."

Theresa sighed. "I should have known it would be a disaster from the very beginning." She turned to Meredith. "Although I hope you won't mention that to your boss."

"Don't worry. I won't," Meredith said lightly, thumbing through a stack of newspaper clippings.

"You work for Vanessa?" Faith asked.

Meredith nodded.

"What do you do for her?" Faith asked.

"I'm her administrative assistant and researcher," Meredith replied. "I answer her e-mail and set up events with bookstores and conferences like this one."

"It must be an interesting job," Faith said.

"It is," Meredith said. "I think the only hard part about it is having to leave my pet parrot at home when we travel."

Watson perked up at the mention of a bird.

"But pets are welcome here," Faith said. "Why didn't you bring your parrot with you?" Privately she was glad, however. She and Watson hadn't been overly fond of the last parrot they'd encountered.

Theresa and Meredith exchanged glances. Obviously, there was something more going on here.

"Vanessa is not exactly a pet person," Meredith admitted. "She finds Ferdinand distracting, and she asked me not to bring him along. Actually, she kind of ordered me not to."

Faith drew in her breath sharply. Not that she should have been surprised considering Vanessa's reaction to Watson earlier in the day. Still, it seemed a bit hard-hearted.

"When Vanessa was in the library this morning, she mentioned that she doesn't like cats," Faith said.

Watson leaped off Faith's lap and retreated to one of the chairs in front of the fire.

Theresa laughed. "Watson seems offended."

"He was indeed," Faith said. "I'll have to make it up to him with some tunaroons."

"Some what?" Meredith asked.

"Tunaroons. My friend Midge Foster owns a pet bakery in town called Happy Tails. She makes unique goodies for pets of all kinds, and she's a vet, so she knows what ingredients are safe for the animals. You should check it out and maybe pick up a treat to take home to Ferdinand. It sounds like he deserves a souvenir."

"That's a good idea," Meredith said. "I'll try to stop by."

"It can't be easy for Vanessa to be surrounded by so many pets," Faith continued. While she had found Vanessa to be a difficult person, she certainly didn't want to show any dislike for one of the guests, especially in front of two others.

"We almost had to change the venue when Vanessa found out the manor welcomed pets," Theresa huffed. "I had to increase her speaker's fee in order to get her to agree to come here. If I had realized how demanding she would be, I would have found someone else to be the keynote speaker."

Meredith fiddled nervously with the rings on her fingers. She was obviously uncomfortable listening to Theresa berate her employer.

"Maybe Vanessa is just under a lot of stress," Faith suggested, trying to give the author the benefit of the doubt. "She mentioned something about needing to make the most of her time."

Meredith sent Faith a grateful smile. "She has been very busy with the Littlest Women series."

Theresa set aside the notebook and reached for another one. "If what Carol Lynn Dodge had to say was true, I can't see that she has all that much work to do," she argued. "It sounded like Vanessa stole the entire series."

"I don't think I should say anything about that," Meredith said. "It feels disloyal for me to gossip about my employer."

"You might as well offer Vanessa's side of the story," Theresa said. "After all, Carol Lynn is more than eager to air her version of events in public."

Meredith bit her lower lip. "I guess you're right. But please don't let Vanessa know you heard anything from me. It may be for her own good, but I doubt she'll see it that way if she finds out."

"I won't tell her. In fact, I'm not planning to even speak to her again for the rest of the conference," Theresa said. "Besides, librarians are known for their discretion, aren't they, Faith?"

"I would never do anything to put you in a difficult position with your employer," Faith promised, though she had to admit that she was more than a little uncomfortable with the situation.

Meredith took a deep breath, then let it out slowly. "Famous authors have this sort of thing happen all the time. If you write enough books, something you publish is bound to resemble someone else's work, if only slightly. There are no new stories, only fresh ways of telling them."

"So Carol Lynn's accusations are unfounded?" Faith asked.

"It's complicated. I understand why Carol Lynn might believe that some of Vanessa's books were based on her own ideas," Meredith said. "Over the years, Carol Lynn has posted a tsunami of fan fiction set in the worlds of Vanessa's books. There were bound to be some similarities after a while."

"I was talking to some of the other attendees after the panel," Theresa said. "They confirmed Carol Lynn's claim that she came up with the idea to write a continuation of the Little Women series ages ago."

"How could they confirm that?" Faith asked.

"They said Carol Lynn posted Littlest Women stories in online forums well before Vanessa announced that she was writing the new series."

"I haven't gone searching for proof," Meredith said. "But I can promise you that Vanessa never copied work or stole ideas from anyone anywhere."

Faith thought the young woman's voice had a ring of truth to it, and she felt inclined to believe her.

Theresa seemed just as willing to let the matter drop, and all three of them turned their attention to the newsletter. The trio sorted through the reference materials and organized them by topic and likelihood of being included in the publication.

Soon Bernadette joined them. "I'm sorry I'm late," she said as she sat down next to Faith.

"Actually, you're right on time," Theresa told her. "We're ready to talk about what kind of stories to include in the newsletter."

The group discussed the types of articles the March sisters might have written. Meredith offered several very creative suggestions, and Bernadette provided invaluable insight as well as a good eye for proofreading and the characters' voices.

Faith was relieved to find that between Meredith and Bernadette, she ended up having to write remarkably little herself.

A couple of hours later, Theresa declared the newsletter complete. "Thank you all for your help." She smiled. "I'm absolutely delighted with this. Even Vanessa will have to admit there's nothing wrong with it."

Faith found herself wondering why Theresa needed to sour their moment of victory with a jab like that.

"I wouldn't be so sure about that," Bernadette responded. "I'd say Vanessa enjoys finding fault. I wouldn't hold my breath waiting for any compliments from her about anything."

Faith was surprised to hear the timid younger woman talking that way about anyone. She wondered if Bernadette had recovered some of her backbone now that the public speaking engagement was behind her. Or maybe Vanessa had been rude enough to provoke even someone as shy as Bernadette into speaking out.

If Vanessa could accomplish that, Faith had an uneasy feeling that the rest of the retreat wouldn't go as smoothly as she'd predicted.

4

Faith felt a shiver of pleasure as she gazed down from the upper level of the Great Hall Gallery. All around the beautiful room, enthusiastic Louisa May Alcott fans clustered in groups, chatting about the day's events and the excitement of the unveiling ceremony.

As Faith started down the stairs, the statue of Dame Agatha Christie caught her eye. It was bathed in a soft glow from the magnificent crystal chandeliers.

"Are you excited about this event?" someone asked from behind her.

She spun around to find Wolfe standing there with his warm smile, and she felt the stresses of the day fade.

Faith smiled in return. "I've been looking forward to this moment ever since we realized we had such a valuable volume in the collection."

Wolfe gestured to the front of the room. "Shall we make sure everything is all set?"

She nodded, and he offered her his arm. She tucked her hand into the crook of his elbow and felt the smooth, tight weave of his evening jacket.

He escorted her slowly through the crowd, smiling and greeting guests as they passed.

Although Castleton Manor was an extraordinary building, Faith knew the real reason it was a success was because of Wolfe and the way he made the guests feel. He thought of every comfort and detail. The reception this evening was just one more example of his gracious hospitality.

They joined Marlene in front of a glass display case draped with a black cloth. The assistant manager was immaculately turned out as always, her fine blonde hair in its classic chignon a perfect complement to her sleek royal-blue sheath dress and strappy silver heels.

"Is everything ready for the ceremony?" Wolfe asked Marlene.

"As you can see, the books are ready to be unveiled," Marlene reported, gesturing to the display case. "Light refreshments will be served afterward. We're just waiting for Ms. Langston to make an appearance."

"I'm so pleased to bring these two incredible volumes together," Wolfe said.

"I am too," Faith said. "It would be wonderful if we could display them together permanently. Has Vanessa agreed to sell you *The Damsel's Fate* by any chance?"

Wolfe frowned. "Unfortunately, no. She told me that she would not consider selling it for any price."

"That's a shame," Faith said. "It would have been an invaluable addition to the collection here."

Vanessa strode toward them. She was even more formally dressed than she had been earlier at the panel. Her peacock-blue evening gown set off her eyes, and a pair of combs held her shiny blonde hair in place.

Marcus Tripp followed a few steps behind. The literary agent had changed out of his sweater vest into an elegant dark suit. Faith noticed that it didn't have any white pet hairs on it.

"Good evening, Ms. Langston, Mr. Tripp," Wolfe said. "Are you ready to start the ceremony?"

"I can't wait," Vanessa said with a grin. "I'm sure the guests feel the same way."

"Let's not keep them in suspense any longer." Wolfe crossed the wide expanse of marble tile and stopped in front of the French doors that framed a breathtaking view of the sea. He cleared his throat and tapped on the microphone beside the display case.

The murmur of conversation faded as the guests gave him their attention.

Wolfe smiled at the assembled audience. "I'm sure all of you devoted fans of Louisa May Alcott share in my excitement in this special moment. To my knowledge, this is the first time *The Maiden's Plight* and *The Damsel's Fate* have ever appeared together as acknowledged works of Louisa May Alcott."

The crowd broke into applause.

Faith felt her heart hammering in her chest at the thought of seeing the volumes together. Judging from the energy in the room, she was not alone in her anticipation.

"And now, without further ado," Wolfe continued, "Ms. Vanessa Langston will do the honors." He stepped back and gestured for the author to approach.

Vanessa glided up to the display case, then smiled at the audience. "It's my pleasure to present these incredible books to you this evening." She whipped the black cloth from the display case with a flourish.

Gasps of delight moved through the crowd, and everyone pressed forward.

Faith slipped through the audience and joined Wolfe near the case. From her vantage point, she was able to see the beautifully preserved volumes quite clearly. As she studied the precious volumes, she felt grateful for this amazing opportunity and the chance to share it with others who cherished the books as much as she did.

After a moment, she decided to yield her place to those who had not yet had a chance to view the rare books, and she headed for the refreshments table.

Brooke had outdone herself once again with a lovely offering of appetizers, fresh fruit, and a wide variety of cheeses. Faith helped herself to several of her favorite hors d'oeuvres—she was pretty sure Brooke had made the salmon puffs and caprese crostini just for her—and added a cluster of plump red grapes.

Brooke sidled up next to her and winked. "Did I see you chatting with Wolfe a few minutes ago?"

Faith was used to her friend teasing her about Wolfe. Brooke claimed that he spent more time at the manor and less time away on business since Faith had started working in the library. "These hors d'oeuvres are delicious," she said, deftly changing the subject.

"Well played," Brooke said. "I'd better get some more fruit. Talk to you later." She scurried out of the room.

Marlene approached the table and inspected the offerings.

"The ceremony went well," Faith remarked to her.

The assistant manager sniffed. "I'm just glad it's over." She lowered her voice. "Ms. Langston has done nothing but complain since she arrived. I don't think there's any pleasing that woman."

Vanessa was even displeased with Marlene's flawlessly efficient service? "I've noticed that," Faith admitted. "I'm hoping her discontent doesn't spread to the other guests."

"I'm sure it won't. It's not often that a guest is disappointed with Castleton Manor," Marlene replied with no small amount of pride.

Another staff member approached at that moment and pulled Marlene away to handle some decision or other.

After snacking and chatting with the guests, Faith headed back up the stairs to enjoy another glimpse of the rare books from the upper level. Only a few guests were still milling about near the volumes.

Faith was peering over the railing to view the books when she heard a gasp. She turned to see Vanessa gaping at Deb Fremont, who had just reached the top of the stairs with her small dog under her arm.

"What are you doing here?" Vanessa demanded.

Deb stopped dead in her tracks and stared at Vanessa. "Attending the conference like everyone else. I'm one of Louisa May Alcott's biggest fans. I can't tell you how excited I was to discover that you were going to be the keynote speaker here."

Rapunzel barked as if in agreement. She wore a silky green jumpsuit with a halter neckline that matched her owner's.

"Stay away from me," Vanessa warned, taking a large step backward.

She must hate dogs as much as she hates cats and birds.

Deb seemed oblivious to Vanessa's discomfort. She closed the distance between them and reached out a hand toward Vanessa.

Vanessa took another giant step and backed into the railing along the upper level. Her arms windmilled as she tried to keep her balance.

Deb lunged at the author.

A look of sheer terror crossed Vanessa's face.

Faith had no idea what was going on, but she instinctively rushed toward the pair. As she neared them, she saw Deb reaching toward Vanessa with her free hand.

Vanessa twisted away and fled down the grand staircase without a backward glance. When she arrived downstairs, she raced through the crowd and paused when she reached the Agatha Christie statue. She looked around as if searching for someone.

Marcus crossed the room and stopped in front of her.

Vanessa said something to Marcus and began jabbing him in the chest with her finger.

Marcus glanced up at the second floor. Faith couldn't be sure, but she thought he was staring at Deb. The woman didn't seem to notice. Her attention was on Rapunzel, who whined and wriggled in her arms. Then Marcus shrugged and started to walk away.

Vanessa rushed out of the room.

"She certainly seems upset, doesn't she?" Deb asked when she'd calmed her dog.

"Do you know what happened to send her hurrying away?" Faith asked.

"Her hair comb had worked itself loose, and I thought she was going to lose it," Deb answered. "When I reached out to fix it for her, she lost her balance. I was afraid she was going to fall over the railing there for a second."

"Why do you think she kept backing away from you?" Faith said. "She appeared frightened to me."

"Maybe she was afraid of Rapunzel," Deb suggested with a shrug. "People have silly fears like that." She kissed the top of her dog's head, then headed down the stairs to join the rest of the guests.

Somehow Faith couldn't imagine that the tiny animal could make anyone feel threatened.

She scanned the crowd again, wondering what had really happened between Deb and Vanessa. She had a feeling there was more to it than met the eye.

She scanned the crowd and saw Deb approaching Marcus. The two began talking. Deb motioned toward the glass case holding the two books, and Marcus shook his head.

As they continued their conversation, Faith replayed the scene between Deb and Vanessa in her mind.

A disturbing thought occurred to her. Had Deb really reached out to save Vanessa?

Or had she attempted to shove the author over the railing?

5

Faith was surprised to hear a commotion as soon as she entered the manor the next morning. Angry voices rang out from the dining room, where the guests were having breakfast. The guests had seemed elated during the unveiling of the two volumes last night, and Faith couldn't imagine what could have occurred since then to cause such a disturbance.

Watson glanced up at her. His expression seemed to say he was not interested in finding out what all the fuss was about. He sauntered away, twitching his bobbed tail ever so slightly as he disappeared down the hall.

Before Faith could go to the dining room to see what was going on, Theresa ran over to her and thrust a pamphlet into her hands. "This is a total outrage."

Faith scanned the articles on the front page and frowned. "This isn't the newsletter we worked on."

"Definitely not."

"Where did it come from?" Faith asked as she perused the rest of the newsletter.

"Someone left a copy of it at everyone's door this morning," Theresa said. "I can't believe it."

"Do you know who could have done this?" Faith asked.

"I have no idea," Theresa said.

Vanessa stormed over to them and waved a copy of the newsletter at Theresa. "How could you circulate such ugly lies and rumors about me?"

"I didn't do it," Theresa protested.

"Don't lie to me," Vanessa snapped.

"Why would you think I'm responsible for this?" Theresa asked.

Vanessa crossed her arms over her chest. "Because you hate me. Obviously the whole thing was your idea, and you're the one who put it together. Or you knew about it and didn't stop it, in which case you're just as guilty."

"I can see why you're upset, but I didn't write it," Theresa said. "Besides, I was working on the real newsletter. I wouldn't have had time to do this one too."

"You could have done it before the conference even started," Vanessa argued.

"It wasn't me," Theresa insisted.

"You'd better hire a lawyer because I'm going to sue you for defamation of character," Vanessa said.

Faith flipped through the newsletter. "There's nothing to prove that this is Theresa's work. What would Theresa stand to gain by spreading this sort of gossip about you?"

"I have no idea," Vanessa said. "But even if she didn't write it, this horrible conference has provided an opportunity for it to be distributed. And I will not tolerate that." She spun around on her heel and stalked away.

Theresa glared after the author.

Faith was a little startled by the intensity in Theresa's gaze. "I'm sure it will all blow over before long," she said, handing the newsletter back to Theresa.

"I've already sunk a lot of my own money into the up-front costs of this conference," Theresa admitted. "What started out as an exciting venture has turned into a total nightmare." She pulled a tissue from her pocket and dabbed at her eyes.

Faith didn't believe for a moment that Theresa was responsible, but she wondered if she might be able to help figure out who was. "Why don't we go to the library and try to make sense of this?"

Theresa nodded.

Faith ushered Theresa to the library, then guided her to the comfortable chairs in front of the fireplace.

Theresa took a seat and opened the newsletter. "Where do we start?"

"Let's take a closer look at what the articles have to say," Faith suggested. "Maybe that will give some kind of a clue as to the author's identity." She sat down in the chair next to Theresa.

"That's a good idea," Theresa said. "But unfortunately, I think most of the articles refer to things that many people, including myself, already knew about." She held the newsletter up so Faith could see it too.

"Let's check it out anyway." Faith scanned the front page and pointed to a story. "What about this one?"

"Mentioning Vanessa fleeing the unveiling ceremony is something anyone who attended the event could have seen for themselves." Theresa sighed. "So that probably doesn't help narrow things down too much."

"I was right near her when it happened. She seemed absolutely terrified," Faith said. "Do you have any idea what could have spooked her so badly about seeing Deb Fremont?"

"Does she have a little dog named Rapunzel?" Theresa asked. "The dog doesn't care for cats if I remember correctly."

"That's her," Faith said.

"Deb has been a member of the Pickwick Club for years, and I've never heard anything negative about her. Do you think Deb could have written the newsletter?"

"She might have," Faith replied. "But there must be other possibilities."

"Like who?" Theresa asked.

"As much as I hate to think it, who would be in a better position to write this kind of thing about Vanessa than her employee?"

"Meredith?" Theresa said.

Faith nodded.

"But Meredith seems like such a sweet young woman," Theresa said. "She was very loyal to Vanessa when she was talking about working for her."

"That might have just been a professional act rather than what she actually thinks," Faith said. "Let's read some of the other articles to see if anything stands out."

"How about this one?" Theresa asked, pointing to a story at the bottom of the page. "It mentions that Vanessa was absolutely paralyzed by writer's block and she was in danger of missing her deadline. Who would know that sort of information?"

"How do we know it's even accurate?" Faith countered. "Someone could have made it up. Although if Vanessa did have writer's block, I doubt she would share that information with anyone but her closest confidants, if she told anyone." She shook her head. "Which brings us back to Meredith."

"But why would Meredith want to jeopardize her job by bad-mouthing her employer?" Theresa asked.

"That's true. And Meredith seems to enjoy the work."

"Vanessa might have confided in Marcus Tripp," Theresa said. "Vanessa's agent would be even more likely to know about things like missing deadlines."

"But what good would it do him to harm Vanessa's reputation?" Faith asked. "Agents want things to go well for their clients. That's how they get paid."

"Considering how badly Vanessa treats everyone, something could have gone wrong and damaged their relationship," Theresa suggested. "Maybe he quit."

Faith gazed at the bright flames dancing in the fireplace. "I can't imagine what it was like for Marcus to work with Vanessa, but he must know how to deal with difficult clients."

"That's a good point."

"And I can't see him purposely causing damage to Vanessa's reputation just because he was angry with her," Faith continued.

"Maybe she flew into a rage and fired him."

"Even if she fired him, he might still make some money from her future earnings, at least for the books he landed the publishing deals for," Faith rationalized. "But that would probably depend on what's in their contract."

Theresa sighed. "It doesn't seem like there's a good reason for anyone to have gone to all this trouble to make a false newsletter. At least not one that I can think of."

"Could it have been created as some kind of publicity stunt?" Faith said.

"Now that you mention it, I suppose it's possible that Vanessa actually wrote it herself."

"She did seem to have a flair for the dramatic when she was onstage yesterday. This would fit in with that quite nicely." Faith thought of something else. "In fact, suing you for defamation of character would bring her into the public eye too."

Theresa nodded. "She believes there's no such thing as bad publicity if it sells more books."

"I'll ask Ms. Russell if there's any chance the newsletter was printed on-site," Faith promised. "I'll let you know what I find out."

Theresa slapped the newsletter down on the arm of the chair. "After what Vanessa put me through, I don't know what I'll do if she's responsible." She jumped to her feet. "I need to get to the bottom of this before it ruins the convention."

Marlene glanced up from her computer when Faith entered her office.

"Have you seen the newsletter?" Faith asked.

Marlene sniffed. "It wasn't exactly what I had in mind when I told Ms. Collins that you would be available to assist her with the project. The entire thing is filled with accusations, rumors, and innuendo. I know you aren't a journalist, but shouldn't you have had better sense than to write something so likely to cause trouble?"

"You can't really believe I'm responsible for the questionable content," Faith said. "That is not the newsletter we worked on yesterday."

"I have to admit, it doesn't really seem to be your style. You've never struck me as a particularly spiteful person." Marlene leaned back in her chair. "So who is responsible for it?"

"Theresa and I were just theorizing," Faith answered. "I wondered if you might have any idea if the newsletter was printed here."

"It certainly could have been. The office center contains everything anyone would need for this kind of a project." Marlene drummed her fingers on the desk. "There are several computers fitted with software used for desktop publishing."

Without an invitation, Faith settled into one of the visitors' chairs across from Marlene.

The assistant manager frowned before continuing. "No one needs to use the actual office center computers, though. The printers are available to use wirelessly from anywhere on the estate. The instructions are available in all the guest suites."

"Is there any way to tell who printed anything or even if the newsletter was printed here for sure?" Faith asked.

"No. I keep telling Wolfe we should track who prints what so we can charge the room, but he prefers to trust our guests to tell us when they've printed something."

"Would you know if any supplies were missing?" Faith said. "Do you keep an inventory?"

"Of course I do," Marlene said, raising an eyebrow. "I'd be a poor manager if I didn't keep an eye on the bottom line. Supplies of every kind impact the finances, especially in a place as large as the manor."

Faith wasn't surprised. Marlene kept her finger on the manor's pulse at all times.

"I'll pull up the file." Marlene tapped on her computer keyboard.

"There should be fifteen reams of copier paper in the supply closet in the office center. I like to keep a large quantity available to guests at all times. It's much easier than having to make a frantic run into town for it."

"Do you mind if I go check on how many reams are actually in there?" Faith asked.

"As long as it doesn't interfere with your responsibilities in running the library," Marlene said.

Faith excused herself and hurried toward the office center.

Sure enough, when she checked the supply closet, there were only fourteen reams of paper. Faith opened the lid on the printer and noticed a blinking light that indicated low ink levels too. It was likely that the culprit had used the office center to produce the controversial newsletter.

Faith glanced around for something that might indicate who had used the office recently.

Unfortunately, there was nothing to point to anyone at all.

The next day dawned bright, sunny, and remarkably warm for a New England March morning. Faith got ready early. She wasn't about to let such beautiful weather go to waste.

Even Watson seemed eager to head outside. Faith found him standing at the front door before she'd even had a chance to slip into her shoes.

After all the uproar the day before, Faith was especially grateful that she didn't need to open the library until after lunch. The tour of Orchard House was that morning, so there would be few people left at the manor.

Faith planned to stop by the Louisa May Alcott book and memorabilia vendor fair. She had been looking forward to checking it out.

If she had time, she might even treat herself to a cup of coffee from the shop at the manor. Faith loved the shop's flavored coffees and the creative daily specials. Then maybe she could take a nice long walk to clear her head.

Faith slid her arms into a fleece jacket and put on a wool hat that Aunt Eileen had knitted for her. It might be warm for March in New England, but that didn't mean it was comfortable enough to go around without outerwear.

As soon as she opened the door, Watson bolted outside. He raced ahead and soon disappeared from view.

She made her way through the extensive gardens that separated her cottage from the manor and paused to enjoy the warmth of the sun on her face. She spotted Watson crouching beneath a spreading rhododendron, his stub of a tail twitching as he watched a pair of blue jays calling to each other from a nearby maple tree.

Faith entered the manor and headed to the salon. Compared to most of the massive rooms in the manor, the salon was cozy with wood floors and pale walls. For this retreat, the salon was set up to accommodate the vendor fair. The booths were open in the mornings before the activities began and during the breaks throughout the day.

As Faith entered the room, she glanced around and smiled. Groups of excited shoppers eagerly sorted through the merchandise for sale.

She stopped at a table covered in T-shirts emblazoned with quotes from the Little Women books as well as Alcott's works for adults. A woman reached past her to grab a mug that said *World's Best Marmee* and show it to her companion.

Faith glanced up to see Dr. Beverly Johnson racing through the room, a panicked expression on her face. She caught up with the other woman. "Excuse me. Is something wrong?" Faith asked.

"All my research is missing!" Beverly blurted out, her eyes wild. "Every folder, every notebook, every scrap of paper. Even my laptop is gone."

6

"That's terrible," Faith said. She felt her stomach tighten at the thought of a theft at the manor.

"I have no idea what I'm going to do," Beverly moaned, twisting her hands.

Faith took a step away from the table and motioned for Beverly to join her in a quieter corner of the room where they were less likely to be overheard. "Where did you last see your things?" she asked.

"I got up early and was using one of the small studies away from the crowds," Beverly explained. "As much as I'm enjoying the conference, I needed a little peace and quiet to get some work done."

"When did this happen?" Faith asked. "Just now?"

Beverly nodded. "I took a break to get a cup of coffee. I left everything set up because I wasn't going to be away very long, but I was delayed by a few attendees who liked one of my classes yesterday. When I returned, everything was gone."

"I'm so sorry about this," Faith told her. "I can see why someone might take your laptop, but I don't understand why someone would take your Louisa May Alcott notes," Faith said. "Is your research valuable to anyone else?"

"I wouldn't think so," Beverly said. "It's of a great deal of interest to me and I expect it will also be to certain parts of academia, but most people wouldn't care about it." She crossed her arms over her chest. "The only person I could imagine taking it is Vanessa Langston."

Faith was surprised by the vehemence in her tone. "Why do you suspect her?"

"I heard she was in the library asking you for resources about Louisa May Alcott's work almost as soon as the convention began."

Faith wondered how Beverly had heard about it, but then she remembered that two retreat guests had been in the library when Vanessa had made the inquiry. One of them must have passed on the information to Beverly.

"What should I do?" Beverly said.

"Under the circumstances, I think you should report it to the assistant manager, Ms. Russell," Faith said, though she dreaded Marlene's reaction. Marlene's first concern would be that the mishap would tarnish the manor's sterling reputation. If a visiting scholar could not feel her work was safe on the property, who could?

"Do you think she'll take the theft of my research seriously?" Beverly asked anxiously. "It isn't as though the items were of great monetary value like *The Maiden's Plight* and *The Damsel's Fate*."

"Ms. Russell takes all guest concerns very seriously," Faith assured her. "I know she'll be eager to help."

"I hope you're right," Beverly said. "I have a contract with a university press for a definitive analysis of Louisa May Alcott's work. Without my research, I don't know how I'll be able to complete the book by my deadline."

"Is there anyone who might wish to keep you from meeting that deadline?" Faith said.

"You mean like a professional rival?" Beverly said, raising her eyebrows.

"That's exactly what I mean."

Beverly slowly shook her head. "I have had nothing but support from my peers."

Faith had another thought. "Is there anything controversial about your research?"

"Some people might consider it controversial," Beverly admitted. "It explores the books Alcott preferred to write. It also analyzes the way that the expectations of gender roles as portrayed in *Little Women* have continued to influence people even today and how Alcott herself would have struggled with that."

"Is it possible that someone could have stolen your research to keep your book from being published?" Faith said.

"Why would anyone want to do that?" Beverly asked.

"Maybe someone doesn't want to believe that Alcott wasn't the kind of woman they would have expected to be behind a book like *Little Women*, and they don't want you publicizing that she preferred to write the more melodramatic tales."

"I suppose it is a possibility," Beverly conceded.

Faith considered the situation. "On the other hand, *The Maiden's Plight* and *The Damsel's Fate* aren't the first such novels to be attributed to Louisa May Alcott. Their existence is wonderful, but it does not come as an earth-shattering surprise. So would stealing your research even make a dent in how they wanted her to be represented?"

"I wouldn't have thought so before, but Alcott still has many ardent fans." Beverly gestured at the devotees of the author who were milling about the room. "And if they're in denial about the truth of who she really was, then maybe they're not thinking rationally anyway."

Faith glanced around. The tables were covered with all manner of Alcott memorabilia and merchandise. Almost all the guests were carrying at least one shopping bag. Clearly, there was still a great deal of money to be made from the stories Alcott had written under her own name, whether she had enjoyed them or not.

Faith wondered if someone had a financial motive for the theft. Maybe it had something to do with the new series Vanessa had been writing. Could Beverly's research cast a pall on it? "Is there any possibility that your book will damage the reputation of Vanessa's Littlest Women series?"

"Somehow I doubt rabid fans of *Little Women* would be influenced by the complexity of Alcott's life," Beverly said.

Vanessa swept into the room with Meredith trailing her.

Immediately a group of fans clustered around the author, clamoring for her attention.

Beverly's face darkened when she saw Vanessa.

"Please let Ms. Russell know what happened," Faith said, trying to draw the woman's attention away from the irascible author. "I'm confident she'll be able to help you locate your research."

"It had better turn up one way or another. I'm not about to sit back and take this quietly," Beverly said. She shot another deadly glare at Vanessa. "No, not quietly at all."

The cat crept around the manor. He took it upon himself to make sure things were on the up-and-up, especially shortly after a new group of guests and their animal companions arrived.

So far, everything appeared to be in order. Even the disagreeable dog had been taken to the kennels, so the cat wouldn't have to worry about running into her. The other animal guests were in the kennels or their owners' suites. And thanks to the cat's diligence, there weren't any rodents or other unwanted creatures roaming the halls or the basement.

As the cat trotted down the corridor, pleased with himself, he spotted a human up ahead.

The cat slowed, pricking up his ears. There was something about the person's movements that he didn't like. He got lower to the floor and followed.

The human reached the door to the back stairwell and glanced around before opening it and ducking inside.

The cat hid behind a plant in the corner of the hall and waited.

A few moments later, the door opened and the person walked out, glanced around once more, then proceeded swiftly in the opposite direction.

The cat approached the door, glad it was still ajar. He nudged it open a little more and scanned the area.

Something glinted in the doorway.

He inched closer. A long, thin substance stretched across the doorway.

The cat wondered what it was and why it was so low to the floor. Even he had to crouch to study it. It certainly wasn't easy to see.

Humans hardly ever noticed anything on the floor, so how would one of them ever see it?

"Good morning," Iris Alden called out brightly. "Gorgeous day, isn't it?" Iris was the delightful manager of the coffee and gift shop. She was a retired museum conservator who had specialized in caring for Early American decorative art.

"It is. And that's why I'm planning to take a long walk." Faith smiled. "But first I need some coffee."

Iris laughed. "Naturally. What can I get you?"

After Faith placed her order, she regarded the eye-catching displays of Louisa May Alcott books and other memorabilia. "That's lovely. Has Marlene made the rounds yet?"

The assistant manager stopped by the shop each morning to critique and make minor changes to Iris's displays. Iris did not appreciate the micromanagement.

Iris grimaced. "Not yet. I'm hoping she'll be too busy with the retreat."

"I'll keep my fingers crossed for you," Faith said with a grin.

Iris grabbed a cup and poured coffee into it. "I heard the commotion yesterday. Did they find out who's responsible for that terrible newsletter?"

"No. It's quite the mystery."

"I hope it gets solved soon." Iris handed Faith the coffee.

"Me too. This conference is getting a little too exciting for me and probably for some of our guests too." Faith paused to inhale the rich scent of coffee, always amazed at how effective it was at making her feel better. "Thank you."

"Anytime. Keep me posted."

"I will," Faith promised. When she left the shop and started down the hall, she heard raised voices.

Beverly and Vanessa stood at the end of the hallway in a heated argument.

Faith didn't want to be privy to this personal conversation. She ducked into a doorway so as not to interrupt them.

"I never would have believed you'd stoop so low as to steal my research," Beverly hissed.

Vanessa put her hands on her hips. "I told you. I don't know what you're talking about. Why would I take your research, anyway?" She snorted. "It's not like I need it."

"I've had it with your arrogance and lies!" Beverly shouted. "Give me back my research, or I'll sue you for every penny you have."

"I don't have to take this. If you won't listen to reason, that's your problem, not mine," Vanessa replied. She turned her back on Beverly and stormed off down the corridor, away from Faith.

Faith couldn't believe what she'd just heard. Was Beverly justified in her bold accusation? Or was Vanessa innocent? After seeing the fake newsletter, Faith wasn't sure she could trust anyone at the conference to tell the entire truth. How could she? She barely knew any of them.

When Beverly told Faith about her missing research, she didn't mention any proof that Vanessa had stolen it, just a suspicion. Had Beverly found some evidence in the short time since Faith had last spoken with her? If so, what could it be?

Faith recalled how rude Vanessa had been to Beverly when they'd appeared together on the panel. What if Beverly had accused Vanessa in an attempt to cast a shadow on the author's character? But why would the professor want to defame a best-selling author? After all, it wasn't as if they were rivals. Even though they both appealed to Alcott fans, Vanessa wrote novels, and Beverly published academic pieces.

Faith continued contemplating Beverly's accusation as she headed to the door.

She was startled out of her thoughts when someone called her name. Marlene. Watson trotted behind her. Faith was somewhat surprised to see them together, as Marlene disliked animals in general and Watson in particular. Maybe she didn't know he was there.

"I'm glad I caught you," Marlene said. "Dr. Johnson informed me of her missing research. Do you know anything about it?"

"She told me that she left her research unattended for a short time, and when she went back, it was gone," Faith replied.

"That's what she told me too." Marlene frowned at Watson as he rubbed against her ankles. "What do you want? Must you do that? I'll have hair everywhere."

The cat sat down next to her and began washing his face.

"I offered to call the police," Marlene continued to Faith. "But I really hate to do that. I don't want them nosing around here and blowing it out of proportion. They'll interrupt the conference, and I'm worried it'll upset the guests. She probably just misplaced her things."

"It doesn't sound like that's what happened," Faith countered.

"I can't think of anyone who'd want to steal those materials. We need to get to the bottom of this before the manor's reputation can be damaged. And we need to figure out where that newsletter came from." Marlene rubbed her temples. "What next?" She met Faith's gaze. "Are you still planning to open the library after lunch?"

Faith nodded.

"Good. Let me know if anything else goes wrong." Marlene strode back down the hallway.

"Would you like to go for a walk?" Faith asked Watson.

The cat meowed.

"Let's go." She held the door open for him.

The pair started off down a path that connected the grounds of the manor with the main road into Lighthouse Bay.

She breathed deeply, inhaling the salty tang of the sea. Overhead, gulls called and reeled. If Faith listened carefully, she could hear the sound of the surf pounding against the rocky shoreline. A sense of well-being filled her, and the tensions of the previous days seemed to slide off her shoulders with each passing step.

The charter bus filled with manor guests passed her and Watson as it headed toward Concord, Massachusetts.

Faith waved at them and hoped they had a good time at Orchard House. She wondered if Vanessa had found the time to join them.

Watson suddenly veered off the path and trotted a few steps, then stopped and glanced over his shoulder as if checking to make sure Faith was following him.

Faith had learned long ago to trust her cat. He had never steered her wrong. As she followed him down the road, she thought she heard a voice call out.

Watson halted at the side of the road and peered down into the deep ditch.

Faith reached him and followed his gaze. She spotted a brightly colored bit of fabric in the brambles at the bottom. "Is anyone down there?" she called.

"Yes! I'm here!" someone cried.

Bernadette Varney lay at the bottom of the ditch.

7

Faith and Watson scrambled down the slope.

"Are you all right?" Faith asked. "Are you injured?"

Bernadette groaned and sat up. "I think I've scraped my leg. It really stings." She lifted her pant leg for inspection, revealing mud and scratches along the length of her calf.

"Oh no. It's not broken, is it?" Faith asked. "Do you think you can stand?"

"I believe so," Bernadette said hesitantly.

"Let's give it a try," Faith said. She extended a hand to the other woman and helped pull her to her feet.

Bernadette cringed. "It feels like I twisted my ankle too."

Faith noticed a damaged bike on the ground. "At least you were wearing a helmet," she said. "Things could have been a whole lot worse."

"But the bike is wrecked, and it's not even mine," Bernadette said. "I borrowed it from the manor."

"Don't worry about that right now," Faith told her. "If you lean on me, can you make it up the hill?"

"I can try," Bernadette said. She draped her arm across Faith's shoulders.

Watson clambered up the embankment and waited for them.

It took several minutes, but Faith and Bernadette finally managed to get to the top of the hill. Faith guided Bernadette to a large rock and helped her sit down.

Faith took her phone out of her pocket and called the manor to send someone to pick them up. After she disconnected, she asked Bernadette, "So how did you end up off the road?"

"I was cycling along, and out of nowhere I heard a car bearing down on me from behind," Bernadette explained. "I swerved to get out of its way and lost my balance. Before I knew it, I had tumbled down the slope. I'm so glad you found me. I left my phone in my suite, and I definitely couldn't have made it back out of the ditch by myself."

Faith motioned to her cat sitting nearby. "The credit goes to Watson. He's the one who found you."

Bernadette smiled. "In that case, thank you, Watson."

The cat lifted his chin with a smug expression.

"Did you see the car?" Faith asked.

Bernadette shook her head. "It all happened so fast. One minute I was minding my own business, enjoying the beautiful weather, and the next I was lying on my back in a patch of brambles. You'd think people would take it easy along these country roads."

Faith had not found that to be the case. Often people from bigger cities saw the quiet country roads around Lighthouse Bay as the perfect place to drive at speeds they never could at home.

"Maybe it was a conference attendee," Faith suggested. "Perhaps one of them missed the tour bus and wanted to be sure to arrive at Orchard House with the rest of the group. The bus passed through here not long before I did."

"I suppose it could have been," Bernadette said.

It suddenly struck Faith as odd that Bernadette hadn't gone on the field trip to Louisa May Alcott's childhood home. "Why did you decide to take a bike ride this morning instead of going to Orchard House? I thought it would be a highlight for all her fans."

Bernadette winced and dropped her gaze. "Although I love Louisa May Alcott, I don't care for large groups," she said quietly. "I needed to recharge my batteries in order to enjoy the rest of the conference."

Faith nodded. Plenty of authors were introverts. "There is a lot planned for the next few days."

"I'm especially looking forward to the costume ball," Bernadette said, her eyes twinkling.

"I hope you'll be recovered by then so you can take a turn around the dance floor," Faith said.

"Even if I don't end up dancing, I'm definitely going to be there."

"You're enough of a fan of dancing to put up with the crowd?" Faith asked.

"No, but I'm writing a book with an important scene set at a ball, and I want to do some research," Bernadette said. "I need to take notes on the experience so I can bring it to life for my readers. Nothing short of being on my deathbed would keep me from being there."

Considering the way things were going, Faith certainly hoped it would not come to that.

A manor employee picked up Faith, Bernadette, and Watson and loaded the damaged bike into the rear of the van.

As soon as they returned to the manor, Watson scampered off.

After thanking the man, Faith put a hand under Bernadette's elbow. "Would you like to see a doctor?"

"No, I'll be fine. I'm just tired and banged up," Bernadette answered. "I want to rest in my room for a little while."

"I'll take you up," Faith offered. She quickly fetched a cup of tea and an ice pack, then escorted Bernadette upstairs to her suite.

"Thank you." Bernadette leaned back in her chair and sighed.

"I hope you feel better soon, and please let us know if you need anything else," Faith said, then left the room and headed downstairs.

Now that she was at the manor, she might as well head to the library and get to work. With how crazy the last couple of days had been, her to-do list had begun to suffer.

She turned a corner and ran into Wolfe. "Oh! I'm sorry."

"Good morning to you too," he said, his voice warm with amusement.

He studied her, and his eyes filled with concern. "You seem a little shaken. Are you all right?"

"Bernadette Varney, one of our guests, had an accident," Faith said.

"Nothing serious, I hope."

"I think she'll be okay. She's resting in her suite."

"Let's sit down, and you can tell me what happened." Wolfe motioned to a pair of chairs set in front of a long window overlooking a formal rose garden.

Faith was more than happy for the opportunity to sit quietly for a few minutes. Her walk had not been nearly as relaxing as she had hoped.

She took a seat, and Wolfe sat in the chair next to her.

Faith gazed out the window for a moment to collect her thoughts. The branches of the rosebushes were still bare, but at least the snow had melted to reveal the lovely brickwork paths and tidy boxwood edging underneath. A lone robin perched on top of a wrought iron trellis. It was a lovely view, and it calmed her enough to share the upsetting tale.

As Faith explained what had happened to Bernadette during her bike ride, she realized that despite the fact that she considered herself to be a self-sufficient person, she appreciated being able to unburden herself to Wolfe. His warm gaze welcomed her confidence and made her feel safe.

He listened quietly, nodding in all the right places until she had completed her story. "Miss Varney was lucky you and Watson found her when you did," Wolfe said. "It's a relatively mild day, but lying on the cold, damp ground for much longer could have given her hypothermia. And the longer she stayed there, the worse things would have gotten."

"Considering how far she fell, I think she was very lucky not to have been seriously injured," Faith said.

"Maybe I should put in a call to Chief Garris and mention what happened," he said.

Faith nodded. "It does seem like more people have been speeding on that road lately. I may have to keep my walks on the estate or on the beach from now on."

"Or perhaps you might welcome a walking companion to help watch for erratic drivers. I'd be happy to provide you with an escort anytime." Wolfe smiled. "All you need to do is ask."

Faith felt a warm glow. He was such a thoughtful man. "I'll keep that in mind," she said, returning his smile.

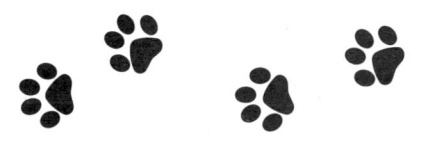

The cat crouched beside a large potted fern and watched his human. He had been following her since she'd left the injured human's room, but he had not made his presence known. He was only there to keep an eye on her. His person had seemed tired and distracted until the nice man asked her to sit with him. She always appeared happier when she spent time with the man.

That was the main reason the cat liked the man. He wanted his human to be content. Besides, it was an undeniable truth that no creature could displace him in his human's affections, so he certainly had nothing to be jealous about.

She and the nice man stood, and the man walked away.

The cat made his move. He sauntered into view and waited for his human to see him standing just ahead of her.

There was something she needed to see.

After Wolfe left for a conference call, Faith continued toward the library, feeling much better.

Watson stepped into her path.

"Where have you been?" she asked.

The cat raced ahead of her, then stopped in the middle of the hall and glanced back over his shoulder as if to urge her on. When he saw her following him, he darted forward again.

Faith wondered where Watson was taking her this time.

When she caught up with him, he was sitting in front of the doorway to a set of back stairs. He meowed and tapped at the door with a paw.

"Why do you want to go in there?" She opened the heavy wooden door, and the feline rushed past her.

As Faith descended the steps, she was grateful that the steep passage was clean and well lit.

The stairs veered around the corner, and Watson disappeared from view.

Suddenly, he let out a series of yowls and meows that reverberated off the walls.

Faith hurried to reach him. "Watson, what is it?" She caught up with him and saw that he was standing stock-still, his back arched and his tail stiff.

Vanessa Langston lay unmoving in a heap at the bottom of the stairs.

8

Faith rushed to Vanessa's side. "Ms. Langston? Vanessa, can you hear me?" As she brushed the hair away from Vanessa's cheek, she noticed the strange angle of her neck. Faith knew there would be no pulse, but she checked anyway.

Vanessa was dead.

Feeling light-headed, Faith sank down onto the floor.

Watson jumped onto her lap and leaned against her.

Faith wrapped her arms around him and forced herself to breathe in and out slowly. She knew she needed to call for help, but at the moment she didn't have the strength to stand.

Watson began kneading her thighs with his paws, purring loudly, and rubbing his face against her chin as if to console her.

Faith scratched his ears gently and soaked in his comfort for a moment. She took a deep breath, then reached for her phone in her pocket and called 911.

She answered the dispatcher's questions as well as she could.

"You're doing great," the kind woman said. "Can you stay on the line with me until help arrives?"

"I wish I could," Faith said, mentally comparing this woman's warmth to the less-than-comforting personality of the person she'd have to phone next. "But I have to call my supervisor and let her know what's going on."

"Okay. I'll have help there as soon as possible."

"Thank you." Faith hung up, took a deep breath, and called Marlene.

"I'm on my way to a meeting," Marlene said without preamble. "Will this take long?"

"I think your meeting will need to be postponed," Faith said with a tremor in her voice.

Marlene must have heard something in her tone. "What catastrophe has struck this conference now? I'm beginning to think it's cursed."

"I just found Vanessa at the bottom of the back stairs," Faith said quietly. "The ambulance and the police are on their way."

"I'll be right there," Marlene said, then disconnected.

Faith carried Watson up the steps and stood at the stairwell door to wait for Marlene.

A few minutes later, Marlene burst through the door. "Show me."

Faith guided Marlene down the stairs and around the corner. They stopped several steps from the bottom.

Marlene stared at Vanessa's motionless body. "Please don't tell me she's dead."

"I'm afraid she is. I think her neck is broken," Faith replied. As she said the words aloud, she felt her stomach lurch. She held Watson tighter, grateful for his comforting presence.

"How did you discover her?" Marlene said.

"Watson led me here," Faith said.

Marlene frowned at the cat as if this were his fault. "I used these stairs just a little while ago, and there was nothing wrong with them. Did you see anything when you came down?"

"No," Faith answered. "I didn't see anything on the steps. They're a bit steep, but the stairwell is well lit and the steps aren't slippery or anything."

"I don't remember anyone ever falling down these stairs."

"I don't either," Faith said. "I can't imagine what happened to Vanessa."

"Did you touch anything?" Marlene asked suddenly.

"I opened the door at the top of the stairs," Faith replied. "I also moved her hair and touched her neck to check for a pulse. I probably ran my hand along the rail or even touched the wall when I discovered her body. I think I was trying to keep myself from fainting."

"I hope you've managed to steady your nerves," Marlene said. "I want you to stay here while I wait upstairs for the police and the paramedics. Perhaps I can get them to use the back entrance to avoid creating such a big scene in front of the guests. Thank goodness most of them are at that tour of Orchard House." She marched up the stairs.

Faith breathed in and out slowly until she felt her heart slow to its regular rhythm. She even felt calm enough to study Vanessa's prone form. She set Watson on the floor and was glad that he didn't approach Vanessa.

In the light from the stairwell, Faith could see a strand of something reflective on Vanessa's pant leg. At first glance, Faith assumed it was one of the victim's own blonde hairs. But somehow it seemed different.

She crouched down next to the body for a closer look. What had appeared to be a hair was something else entirely. A length of fishing line clung to the dead woman's pant leg. She peered closer. Attached to each end of the fishing line was a tiny brass nail.

Watson rose on his hind legs and placed his front paws on her thigh.

Faith sank to the floor and gathered him into her lap. Try as she might, she couldn't take her eyes off the body.

There was no doubt in her mind. Vanessa's fall had not been an accident.

Police Chief Andy Garris was the first person to arrive on the scene.

Faith took comfort in the fact that he was the one in charge. She had always found him to be fair and sensible as well as intelligent. He understood that even though he had seen a great deal of trauma and crime in his line of work, most of the citizens of Lighthouse Bay had not.

She was slightly embarrassed for him to find her slumped on the floor in front of the door to the stairwell with Watson clutched to her chest. After discovering the fishing line, Faith had wanted to put some distance between her and Vanessa's body, so she'd climbed the stairs and sat down to wait for help.

"Are you all right?" the chief asked.

Faith nodded.

Garris helped her to her feet and escorted her to an empty room. "Have a seat." He steered her to a chair at a small table near the heat vent.

Watson curled up on Faith's lap, and Faith stroked his back, grateful that her cat was sticking close.

"Can you tell me what happened?" Garris asked gently. He pulled a notepad and a pen from his pocket.

"Watson led me to the back stairs, and we found Vanessa lying on the floor at the bottom of the steps," Faith explained.

He began taking notes. "What did you do?"

"I rushed down the stairs to help her, but I knew immediately that she hadn't survived the fall."

"How did you know that?" the chief asked.

"I could tell her neck was broken," Faith said, her stomach rolling at the memory. "But I checked for a pulse to be sure."

"It must have given you quite a shock," Garris remarked.

"It did."

"Did you try to move the body?"

Faith shook her head. "I left her exactly how I found her except for brushing her hair away from her face when I felt for a pulse."

"What do you think happened to Ms. Langston?"

"The stairs are quite steep, so I assumed she had simply lost her footing."

"That seems logical," he agreed. "Did you see anything unusual as you came down the stairs?"

"Not on the stairs," Faith said slowly.

"What did you see?" The chief's voice was calm, but he stopped scribbling notes and gave Faith his full attention.

"While Marlene went upstairs to wait for help to arrive, I stayed with Vanessa's body," she answered. "I noticed something on the leg of her trousers."

"What was it?"

"A length of fishing line with a small nail on each end," Faith said. Her stomach knotted again.

"Do you feel up to showing me?" Garris said as he slid his notepad and pen into his pocket.

Faith nodded.

Watson pressed his head against her neck, then leaped to the floor and began grooming himself.

Faith stood and was relieved to find her legs felt much sturdier than they had been a few moments earlier.

She followed Chief Garris to the stairwell, where Officers Jan Rooney and Bryan Laddy had cordoned off the area and stood waiting for instructions from the chief.

Faith took the lead on the way down the stairs and forced herself to look at Vanessa's lifeless body once more. "Right there," she said, pointing.

"I see it," the chief said. He motioned to Officer Rooney. "Check out the staircase, and see if you can find a reason for that fishing line to be in here."

Officer Rooney raised an eyebrow. "Will do, Chief."

Garris turned to Faith. "Let's go back to that room and sit down," he suggested gently.

They retook their seats at the table just as Marlene entered and sat next to Faith.

A few minutes later, Officer Rooney walked in. "They would be very easy to miss if you weren't searching for them, but there are two small holes in the walls on either side of the threshold to the stairs. I'd guess they're the right size for the nails attached to the fishing line."

"So someone intentionally put the line there to make sure Ms. Langston would trip and fall," the chief concluded.

"It certainly appears that way," Officer Rooney said.

"I'd say we're going to have to investigate this as a homicide," the chief said.

Faith's mind raced with the possibilities. Anyone could have come along and tripped over that fishing line. She shivered. "Even if it wasn't an accident, how do we know Vanessa was the intended victim?"

"We don't yet, but we have to start somewhere," Garris said. "We'll begin by digging into the victim's background. Can you think of anyone who might have wanted Ms. Langston out of the way?"

"I hate to say it, but Vanessa was not the most likable person," Faith admitted. "It seemed she had issues with several of the guests."

The chief removed his notepad and pen from his pocket again. "Could you provide me with any names?"

"I feel uncomfortable spreading gossip about our guests," Faith said.

"It's your duty to cooperate. You know that," Garris said. "I'm sure Mr. Jaxon and Ms. Russell will be eager for you to assist us in any way that you can."

Faith glanced at Marlene.

"Usually our guests value discretion, but an active police investigation precludes that," Marlene told her.

Faith took a deep breath and tried to recall everything she could that might be relevant. "Vanessa was the keynote speaker for the Louisa May Alcott conference being held here this week. She seemed to have several enemies from the beginning, and she just created more as she went."

"Like who?" Garris asked.

"She was dismissive of the other two experts on a panel with her the first day of the conference," Faith said. "Their names are Dr. Beverly Johnson and Bernadette Varney."

The chief wrote the names down in his notepad.

"At that panel, Carol Lynn Dodge publicly accused Vanessa of stealing her idea for her new series," Faith added.

"Is that everyone?"

"Vanessa gave the conference organizer, Theresa Collins, a hard time and threatened to sue her."

"Sue her?" Garris repeated.

"Yes, for defamation of character," Faith responded. "A fake newsletter criticizing Vanessa went around yesterday, and she blamed Theresa for it."

"Anything else?" the chief asked.

"I overheard Vanessa arguing with Beverly this morning."

"What were they arguing about?" Garris said.

"Beverly accused Vanessa of stealing her research and her laptop," Faith said.

"Is that the same material you reported missing earlier today?" the chief asked Marlene.

"Yes, but I still believe it will turn up. I imagine it was simply misplaced."

"Let's get back to the argument," Garris said. "What did Ms. Langston say about Dr. Johnson's accusation that she stole her property?"

"She denied it," Faith answered. "And then she marched off."

"Can you think of anything else that might be helpful?" the chief asked.

"I believe Vanessa was afraid of Deb Fremont, one of the conference attendees." A stab of regret pierced Faith as she said it. Deb had seemed like a nice woman when they had met earlier. But so had the other women Faith had mentioned. She hated to cast suspicion on any of them, but she had been fooled before by people who had appeared to be harmless.

"What reason would the victim have had to be afraid of Ms. Fremont?" Garris asked.

"I really have no idea," Faith admitted. "I just know that Vanessa nearly fell over a railing on the second floor trying to get away from her."

"How did that happen?" the chief asked, making more hurried notes.

Faith shrugged. "When Vanessa saw Deb, she backed up so far and so fast that she almost fell over the second-floor railing in the Great Hall Gallery. I guess she wasn't paying attention."

"Was there anything said that would explain Ms. Langston's extreme reaction?"

"I didn't think so. Vanessa asked Deb what she was doing at the manor, and Deb said she was an Alcott fan. Then Vanessa nearly went over the railing trying to get away from her. The second she recovered, she raced from the room." The whole scene sounded preposterous to Faith when she described it to the chief. "Vanessa doesn't like animals and Deb had her little dog with her, so I wondered if maybe that was it, but it still seems like a pretty dramatic reaction."

"It didn't appear that Ms. Fremont threatened the victim in any way?" the chief continued.

"Not that I could tell," Faith said. "Deb reached toward Vanessa just before she backed into the railing."

"Do you know why?"

"She told me afterward that one of Vanessa's hair combs was coming loose and she intended to secure it."

"Did anyone else witness what happened?" Garris said.

"I'm sure I couldn't have been the only one," Faith said. "Not to speak ill of the dead, but Vanessa seemed to enjoy causing a scene."

"Are you suggesting she might have been feigning fear to attract attention?"

"I didn't know her well enough to say for sure," Faith said. "I think you'd be better off asking Meredith Harris or Marcus Tripp for insight into her personality."

"Who are they?" Garris asked. "Conference attendees?"

"Meredith is Vanessa's assistant, and Marcus is her literary agent." Faith paused. "At least they were."

"I'll need to speak to both of them as soon as possible," the chief said. "Are they staying here at the manor?"

Faith nodded. "But I'm not sure where they are at the moment. We don't exactly keep tabs on guests. They could be on the grounds or really anywhere in the area. Most of our guests left for a tour of Orchard House in Concord this morning."

"When are they due at the manor?" Garris asked.

"They stopped for lunch at a tearoom on the way back," Marlene spoke up. She checked her watch. "I expect them to return within the hour."

Faith realized that all the conference attendees were possible suspects. She wondered how the chief could narrow down the long list. "Do you need to know who was here and who wasn't when Vanessa died?"

The chief frowned. "Unfortunately, that may not make much difference. The murderer could have stretched the fishing line across the threshold and then boarded the bus along with everyone else." He closed his notepad. "It may come down to motive more than opportunity."

As Faith realized the malice that must be involved in setting a trip wire in the stairwell, she wasn't sure she would ever feel safe again.

9

Faith still felt dazed when Chief Garris finished questioning her and rejoined his officers at the crime scene.

"I need to let Wolfe know what happened," Marlene told her. "Unless he or the chief says otherwise, we're operating as usual, all right?"

Faith wasn't sure how she could do anything as usual right now, but she managed to nod.

Marlene stood as if this were just another day, just another crisis, and left the room with purposeful strides.

Faith walked down the corridor with Watson at her side. She slipped out a side exit, then drew in a few deep, calming breaths of fresh air. All she wanted to do was retreat to her cottage and hide with her cat, her books, and her tea for the rest of the day. Maybe she could at least sequester herself there to eat her lunch before she had to open the library.

"Miss Newberry, is it true?" a male voice called.

Faith stopped and glanced over her shoulder.

Marcus Tripp hurried toward her. A little white Maltese on a leash struggled to keep up with him.

Faith's heart sank. Her time alone in her cottage would have to wait. She did her best to appear welcoming as she faced the red-cheeked older man. If he didn't know that Vanessa was dead, it wasn't her place to tell him. Besides, she knew that a formal announcement would be made to the guests soon. "Is what true?"

"The news about Vanessa, of course," Marcus said. If anything, the man's rosy cheeks were even more flushed than usual. "There are police cars everywhere, and people are saying that Vanessa is dead."

Faith briefly debated over whether to confirm it. On one hand,

Marlene might not be happy with her if she did, as the assistant manager would want to be in control of communications about the grisly situation. On the other hand, confirming it now would hopefully forestall rumors about other unsavory reasons for the police to be there.

"I'm so sorry to tell you this, but Vanessa is indeed gone," Faith said gently.

"How do you know?" Marcus waved his arms, inadvertently tugging on the dog's leash. "Are you sure?"

His small dog appeared to be equally agitated. Faith didn't know if it was responding to its owner's emotional state or if it was uncomfortable because Marcus kept yanking on the leash as he made wild gestures.

She took pity on the dog and rested a steadying hand on Marcus's arm. "Yes, I'm sure. I was the one who found her body."

Marcus's shoulders slumped. He shook his head slowly. "I can't believe it. How could this possibly happen? Vanessa was so vibrant. How can she be gone?"

"I know," Faith said. "It's a terrible shock, but the police here are very good. They'll find out what happened to her."

The little dog seemed to calm, and Faith bent down and held out the back of her hand for it to sniff.

"This is Maisie," Marcus said.

The dog wagged her tail at the mention of her name.

"She's adorable," Faith said. She was relieved to note that Maisie seemed to take Watson's presence in stride.

For his part, Watson pointedly ignored the dog.

"I was supposed to meet with Vanessa this morning," Marcus went on, "but she never arrived. I feel terrible to think that I was angry with her for not keeping our appointment."

"Is that why you didn't go on the field trip to Orchard House?" Faith asked.

"That was part of it. I didn't want to run into her when I was so annoyed with her," Marcus said. He leaned forward and lowered his voice. "But the truth is, I've had all the Louisa May Alcott that I can stand for one lifetime."

"You're not an Alcott fan?" Faith asked.

"It's not that," Marcus said. "It's just that a steady diet of anything becomes unappetizing after a while. I guess I should have been grateful that Vanessa didn't feel that way."

"I'm so very sorry," Faith said.

"I've known Vanessa for many years, and she's been my client for her entire career." Marcus frowned. "It's impossible to imagine someone so full of life being snatched from us in the blink of an eye."

It was clear that Marcus was genuinely upset. But secretly Faith had to wonder if he was more distressed at the loss of life or at the loss of profits from future books. She wondered if Marcus had gotten along any better with the difficult woman than anyone else seemed to. There was only one way to find out.

"Not to speak ill of the dead, but you're one of the only people I've heard who had anything positive to say about Vanessa as a person," Faith said. "I realize many people enjoyed her books, but almost no one I've spoken to seemed to like her company. As her agent, I suppose you saw another side of her."

"I know she rubbed most people the wrong way, but we got along well," Marcus said. "For some reason, we seemed to understand each other. Although perhaps I wasn't always as understanding as I should have been." He let out a deep sigh.

"It sounds as though you're thinking of something specific," Faith said.

"As a matter of fact, there is something I deeply regret," Marcus said. "At the time, it seemed like another one of Vanessa's typical overreactions."

"If you don't mind my asking, what happened?" Faith said.

"One of the things people didn't particularly care for about Vanessa was her inclination toward the dramatic. She tended to blow things out of proportion. I learned to respond to her fits with comfort and reassurance, and I could usually get her to calm down. But now I realize that her instincts were far better than my own."

"Why don't you tell me about it?" Faith said. She motioned to a bench in a patch of sun. It was nestled against a bank of rhododendron bushes and tucked away from the main path. If any spot would invite confidences, that would be it.

Marcus followed her to the bench and sat down. He scooped up his dog and set her on his lap. "There you go, Maisie. That should keep your feet warmer." He rubbed the little dog's ears, then planted a kiss on the top of her head.

Maisie made a contented grunting sound as if she concurred.

Faith could see that Maisie gave Marcus the same sort of support in times of trouble that she got from Watson.

"So what's troubling you?" Faith asked as Watson settled down on her lap.

"Some time ago, Vanessa became convinced that Deb Fremont had crossed the line from fan to stalker," Marcus said.

Faith was startled at the news, but it explained why Vanessa had had such a strong reaction to Deb the other night. "From what I've seen of Deb at the conference, she doesn't seem dangerous."

"That's exactly how I felt," Marcus admitted. "But Vanessa was upset by Deb's attention. When she told me about her worries, I assumed she was overreacting. Now I regret not being more concerned."

"What did Deb do that bothered Vanessa?" Faith asked.

"She writes a blog about Vanessa's work and maintains a fan club on social media, which is pretty normal. But she also sent fan mail and gifts directly to Vanessa's home instead of to the publisher. She came to every one of Vanessa's appearances no matter where they were, even traveling across the country to get there."

"That seems excessive, even for one's favorite author," Faith said. "I can see why Vanessa might have found it a little creepy."

"I tried to tell Vanessa that it was the price of success, but she complained that it was extremely disturbing."

"Did you do anything about it?" Faith asked.

Shame covered his face. "I didn't take Vanessa seriously because I thought she was actually enjoying the drama of it. She was like that."

Faith couldn't blame him. She had gotten the same impression from Vanessa, and she had hardly known the woman.

A cloud passed over the sun and left the bench momentarily in shadow.

Faith felt chilled by more than the patch of shade as she considered the situation. Deb seemed friendly and pleasant, but Faith knew that sometimes appearances could be deceiving. "Do you know if Deb ever threatened Vanessa? Or if she did something to suggest that she would turn violent?"

"Never," Marcus answered. "Which was one of the reasons why I advised Vanessa to simply grin and bear it. But now I fear I did the wrong thing."

"What do you mean?" Faith asked.

Marcus sighed. "Vanessa told me she was going to get a restraining order against Deb, but I told her that the publicity from seeking a restraining order would do her far more harm than good. I said that she didn't want to risk alienating her fans, especially when she was launching a new series. I mean, Deb hadn't done anything really wrong, so it would have seemed that Vanessa didn't want a relationship with her fans. And contrary to popular belief, you can have bad publicity."

"You have to tell the police how Vanessa felt about Deb's attention," Faith said.

Marcus looked hesitant.

"As her agent, you owe it to Vanessa to speak up," Faith pressed. "After all, isn't it an agent's responsibility to advocate for his clients?"

Marcus exhaled slowly. "I suppose you're right. Sadly, Vanessa can't speak for herself anymore, can she?"

Faith bit back a gasp. Had Marcus come close to the motive for the author's murder?

Did someone kill Vanessa so she could never speak again?

10

Faith and Watson made a welcome retreat to the cottage that evening. It had been a long, frightening day, and she attempted to settle her nerves with a Dorothy L. Sayers novel, a cup of hot tea, and Watson cuddled up next to her.

As much as she loved Sayers, she had to admit that it hadn't been the best choice, as the fictional murder mystery kept reminding her of her real-life murder mystery. After an hour of holding the book open but staring off into space as her brain mulled over what she knew about Vanessa's death, she gave up and went to bed.

She didn't think she'd ever get to sleep, but she was so exhausted that she dropped right off, and the next thing she knew it was morning. As they walked to the manor, Watson kept glancing up at her as though concerned for her well-being.

She smiled at her cat. "I'm fine. You don't have to worry."

She didn't think he believed her.

When they slipped inside the manor, Faith could hear guests' subdued conversations. The news of Vanessa's tragic and unexpected death had surely spread throughout the group. She expected many of the guests would wish to find solace at the library. She knew that was what she would want to do.

She headed toward the library while Watson took off in the opposite direction.

Faith was surprised to see Beverly standing next to the library door. "Good morning. I'm sorry to keep you waiting."

"It's fine," Beverly said. "I was up early again this morning, and I wanted to talk to you right away."

"Of course. What can I do for you?" Faith unlocked the door and gestured Beverly inside.

"I was wondering about *The Damsel's Fate*."

"What about it?" Faith asked as she stowed her purse in her desk.

"Vanessa offered to loan the book to me," Beverly replied, "and I'd like to see it."

"I'm sorry, but the book isn't in the library."

"Where is it then? I thought it would be under lock and key."

"Ms. Langston preferred to keep it with her at all times," Faith explained.

"What did she plan to do with it?" Beverly scoffed. "Tuck it under her pillow?"

"I really don't know. When did she offer to lend it to you?"

"Yesterday morning." Beverly frowned. "Although I think she said it simply to placate me after I accused her of stealing my research."

"Have you found your research yet?"

"No, but I reported it to Ms. Russell. She agreed to inform the police and promised to keep me posted."

"I hope it's returned to you soon."

"I do too. I really don't know what I'll do if it's gone forever," Beverly said. "In the meantime, I was hoping to see Vanessa's book despite her unfortunate accident."

"As much as I'd like to help you, I simply don't know where the book is," Faith said.

"It's very valuable," Beverly declared. "If I were you, I'd track it down and put it somewhere for safekeeping immediately."

"Is there anything else I can do for you?" Faith asked.

Beverly shook her head. "I really should get going. Please let me know when you find the book," she said, then left.

Faith realized that she had been so preoccupied with Vanessa's death that she hadn't even considered the whereabouts of her book. She assumed it was still in Vanessa's room, but Beverly had made a good point about locating it. She needed to check with Marlene to make sure it was okay for her to go into Vanessa's suite, though.

She called Laura and asked if she would be available to watch the library for a little while. The young woman readily agreed.

Faith began shelving books as she waited for Laura. She tried to keep herself occupied with the task, but she couldn't help wondering about *The Damsel's Fate*.

Ten minutes later, Laura breezed into the library.

"Thanks for taking care of the library while I step out," Faith said.

"It's my pleasure," Laura said. She pointed at the book cart. "Would you like me to finish shelving those?"

"That would be great. Thanks," Faith said. "I'll be back soon."

"There's no rush. I have some extra time this morning."

Faith left the library and went in search of Marlene. She found the assistant manager in the laundry room, where she was grilling a beleaguered young woman about her generous use of laundry detergent. When Faith interrupted them, the staffer appeared relieved, but Marlene didn't seem ready to end her tirade.

"What is it now?" Marlene said. "I'm sure you're aware that this has been an extremely trying couple of days."

"May I speak with you privately?" Faith asked. "I'm afraid it's rather important."

Marlene pursed her lips and gave Faith a terse nod. She scowled at the laundress. "We have more to discuss later."

Faith followed Marlene out the door.

"All right, what's so important? Is this about Ms. Langston's death?" Marlene tapped her foot impatiently, and the sound bounced off the walls of the long corridor.

Faith took a deep breath and mentally prepared herself for Marlene's expected reaction. "No. Something else has come up. I've just been approached by Beverly with a request to see Vanessa's copy of *The Damsel's Fate*. She claims that Vanessa gave her permission to borrow it for her research."

"What does that have to do with me? You're the librarian." Marlene started to walk away.

Faith hurried after her. "I may be the librarian, but the book doesn't belong to the Castleton Manor library. It belonged to Vanessa."

"Which means it has even less to do with me. Why are we having this discussion?"

"As Beverly made a point of reminding me, the volume is extremely rare and very valuable. Shouldn't we locate it and put it somewhere safe?"

Marlene snorted.

Faith tried again. "We wouldn't want the manor to be held responsible for it going missing, would we?"

That got Marlene's attention. The assistant manager stopped and spun around to face Faith. "No we would not. You didn't see the book with her body, did you?"

Faith pictured Vanessa crumpled at the foot of the stairs. There had been nothing unusual except the fishing line, and she had seen no sign that the book had been beneath her body. She doubted very much that she would have missed something like that even under the distressing circumstances. And if the book had been there, surely whoever had moved Vanessa would have spotted it and said something.

"I wouldn't swear to it in court, but I'm quite certain the book was not with her," Faith said.

Marlene patted the key ring at her waist. "I have the key to her room. Come with me, and we'll check it together."

When they reached Vanessa's suite on the second floor, Marlene ignored the *Do Not Disturb* sign on the doorknob. She turned the key smoothly in the lock and opened the door.

The curtains were closed, and the air felt stuffy. Faith assumed the housekeepers had not been inside to clean for the entire duration of Vanessa's visit.

The bed was unmade, and various articles of clothing were strewn about the room. Dresses and skirts and blouses were draped over the backs of chairs, the settee at the foot of the bed, and even over one of the lamps. Faith plucked the skirt off the lamp. It was a fire hazard after all.

The dressing table was cluttered with tubes of lipstick, jars of lotions, and bottles of nail polish. A laptop, several notebooks, and a few pens covered the desk that was positioned in front of a long set of windows overlooking a vast sweep of lawn.

Marlene glanced around. "Not very tidy, was she? I don't know how we're going to find anything in this mess."

Faith silently agreed.

Marlene walked over to the armoire positioned against the far wall and yanked open the doors. She slid the hangers across the pole and felt the pockets of the clothing hanging there.

"Are you sure it's okay for us to go poking through Vanessa's personal belongings without permission from the police?" Faith said.

"The chief released the room to me. It's not open to the public yet, but he said I could come in here if I needed to." She went over to the bed and felt under the mattress.

Resigned to search the entire room even though it felt strange, Faith headed for the desk and rifled through the drawers. There was nothing in any of them except the stationery provided by the manor.

She didn't find anything of interest hidden among the articles of clothing in the drawers of the dresser. Then Faith peered under the sofa and the bed. She lifted cushions, papers, and pillows, and even checked inside an empty suitcase she found in the corner.

There was no sign of Beverly's laptop or research, though she hadn't expected to find them in Vanessa's room. She also didn't see *The Damsel's Fate*.

But Faith did spot the resource materials she'd gotten for Vanessa. She would return them to Eileen this evening at their meeting of the Candle House Book Club. She was looking forward to meeting with Brooke, Midge, and her aunt even more than usual.

"I hate to say it, but I don't think the book's in here," Faith concluded. "I only hope it hasn't been stolen."

"I knew it was a mistake to host that unveiling ceremony,"

Marlene groused as she sorted through a pile of books and papers on the nightstand.

Faith didn't agree that the ceremony had been a mistake, but she was becoming more and more concerned that theft was a real possibility. She scanned the room once more. "What do we do now?"

Marlene stepped back from the nightstand and put her hands on her hips. "Is there any chance Vanessa gave the book to someone else for safekeeping?"

Faith felt a slight flutter of hope. "We could ask her assistant, Meredith. Or she might have given it to her agent, Marcus."

"We need to inform Wolfe about this before we speak to anyone else," Marlene said. "We don't want to start any rumors or reveal that the book is missing. People might get the idea that if they find it they can keep it."

Faith thought that was a pretty pessimistic view, but she nodded. "Do you want to tell him, or should I?"

"You do it," Marlene said. "I need to get back to the laundry room to finish my conversation with that new hire."

"I'll let you know what Wolfe has to say about it," Faith said. "And go easy on the new employee. I'm sure she'll be great about the detergent from now on."

"Do I tell you how to shelve books?" Marlene demanded. "Now come on. I need to lock up."

Faith grabbed the resource materials and hurried out the door. When she shut it behind her, she could have sworn she saw a flash of movement as someone ducked around the corner.

She shivered at the feeling of being watched and wondered why anyone might be skulking around the hallway.

Was another player trying to track down Vanessa's copy of *The Damsel's Fate*?

11

When Faith returned to the library, she was glad to see that Laura had things well in hand. She was assisting one of the guests, and several other patrons browsed the stacks. There were even a few guests reading in the chairs by the fireplace.

Faith waited until Laura had finished explaining the mystery section to the guest and joined her. "I'm sorry it took a little longer than I expected," Faith said. "Thanks again for filling in."

"Don't worry about it. Everything's fine," Laura said. "But I'd better get going. If I fall behind on housekeeping, Marlene will have my hide. Talk to you later."

After Laura was gone, Faith phoned Wolfe and asked him to meet her in the library. She filed some papers and straightened up her desk while she waited for him to arrive.

By the time Wolfe entered the library, it was empty. Faith had checked out books for the patrons, and the rest had left to attend the morning sessions.

Faith walked over to greet him. "Thanks for coming by."

"I apologize for not checking in with you sooner," Wolfe said, "but I've been busy speaking with the police and fielding questions from the other guests."

"I understand," Faith said.

"Let's sit down," Wolfe said, gesturing toward the chairs in front of the fireplace.

Faith took a seat next to Watson, who was curled up in a chair and snoozing contentedly. The cat yawned and stretched, then stared at Faith. Obviously, he didn't appreciate her interrupting his nap.

"I didn't even see you over here," Wolfe said to Watson. He

scratched the cat behind the ears.

Faith smiled as Watson purred. "At least someone knows how to appease him when I commit grave offenses like waking him."

"I try." Wolfe sat down in the chair on the other side of Faith and studied her face. "Finding Vanessa's body must have been a horrific experience. How are you doing?"

"I'm okay," Faith said. "But I do have a question for you, and I hope you'll have some good news."

"I'll try to help," Wolfe said. "What do you need?"

"Did Vanessa ask you to take charge of *The Damsel's Fate* after the unveiling ceremony?" She held her breath as she waited for his answer.

"No, she didn't. I offered to keep it locked in the case with *The Maiden's Plight*, but she refused just like she had before."

"Did she say why?" Faith asked, hoping her tone wouldn't convey her frustration at the author's irresponsible behavior with regard to the book. After all, it wasn't her place to decide what someone else should do with their possessions, but it bothered Faith when valuable books were not properly cared for.

"She told me she was using the book as inspiration for her work in progress and it helped her to have it at hand," Wolfe responded. "She seemed to think such precautions were unnecessary and even a bit paranoid."

"Then I think we have a problem," Faith said.

Wolfe raised his eyebrows. "What is it?"

"Marlene and I just checked Vanessa's room. The book is nowhere to be found."

"Are you sure?" Wolfe asked. "Did you search absolutely everywhere?"

"We were very thorough," Faith assured him. "The book is not in her room."

"I suppose I had better inform the police," Wolfe said. He removed his phone from his pocket and hesitated. "Before I call the chief, would you ask Vanessa's assistant and her agent if she entrusted it to either of them for safekeeping?"

"Of course," Faith said. "I was wondering the same thing."

"Thank you. I'd hate to bother the police until we know for sure that the book is missing. They have enough on their plates at the moment."

"There is something else. Beverly's laptop and all her research is missing." Faith filled him in on what had happened and how Beverly had accused Vanessa of stealing the materials.

"That's terrible. Do you have any ideas as to where her things could be?"

Faith shook her head.

"Thank you for telling me about all this. It certainly isn't turning into the event everyone had hoped for. Keep me updated, please." Wolfe checked his watch. "If that's it, I'd better get back to work."

She gave him as much of a smile as she could muster. "Yes, that's it for now. I'll let you know what I discover. I hope Meredith or Marcus can help." Despite her optimistic words, she had a sinking feeling that the book would not be so easy to find.

"I'm sure everything will work out. It usually does," Wolfe reassured her. He gave her one of his warm smiles and left.

Fortunately, the guests were attending sessions, so the library was still empty, except for Watson, who had resituated himself and gone back to sleep. It was the perfect time to see if she could chase down a wayward book. Faith locked the library door and hurried down the hall.

She found Meredith in a small alcove at the back of the manor. The younger woman was hunched over a laptop, her fingers flying over the keys. She practically jumped out of her skin when Faith called her name.

"I'm so sorry to have startled you," Faith said. "Although I'm not surprised if you're a little jumpy after all that's happened."

Meredith sighed. "I don't feel like myself. I think I'm still in shock." She glanced around the alcove. "Do you need this space? I can go somewhere else."

"Actually, I was looking for you," Faith said. "I was hoping you could answer a question for me."

Meredith shrugged. "Go ahead, but I don't think I have any answers. I certainly couldn't help the police much when they questioned me yesterday."

"This won't take long," Faith said. "And then you can get back to whatever it is you're working on."

"I'm just sending out some e-mails," Meredith said. She leaned back in her chair. "What is it that you wanted to ask me?"

"Did Vanessa ask you to take care of her copy of *The Damsel's Fate*?"

The color drained from Meredith's face. "She certainly did not. Vanessa wanted it in her own room where she could dip into it now and again. She said it was inspiring her as she wrote the Littlest Women series."

Faith suddenly realized something odd about that. "Did that make any sense to you since that sort of novel has nothing in common with *Little Women*?"

"I never really thought about it," Meredith said. "Why are you asking me about the book?"

"Because it's been brought to our attention that we don't know precisely where it is at the moment, and we wanted to be sure that it's safe," Faith said.

Meredith raised her eyebrows. "Are you saying it's been stolen?"

"I don't know that yet."

"Have you checked her room?" Meredith asked.

"It's been searched from top to bottom," Faith said, "but it's not there."

"Have you talked to Mr. Jaxon?" Meredith asked. "Maybe Vanessa asked him to put it in the safe after the unveiling ceremony."

"He assures me that she didn't despite the fact that he offered," Faith said. "Is there any possibility she could have asked Marcus to keep it for her?"

"I doubt it. If she didn't ask me, I don't believe she would have asked anyone else."

"Did she ever worry that someone might try to steal the book from her?" Faith asked.

"Vanessa was quite immature in some ways and tended to think that people who were more responsible were worrywarts," Meredith said. "I could never convince her to take anything more seriously than she did."

"Was it common knowledge that Vanessa was careless with the book?" Faith said.

"It might have been," Meredith said. "She wasn't always discreet."

"Could she have had the book with her when she died?" Faith asked.

"I don't know, but it's possible," Meredith replied. "Do you think someone killed her in order to steal *The Damsel's Fate*?"

"Maybe," Faith said. "I'll let you get back to work. Thanks for your time."

"No problem. Please keep me posted on what you find out."

Faith agreed.

As she walked away, she wondered if Meredith was right about the killer's motive.

Then a chilling thought struck her. What if the thief planned to steal *The Maiden's Plight* next? The book was currently locked up in the library—the library in Faith's care.

Was she standing in the way of a killer?

Faith found Marcus sitting at a table in the breakfast room. His dog, Maisie, was perched in the chair next to him.

Despite the worries of the day, Faith was still able to appreciate the sunlight streaming through the tall windows and warming her skin as she made her way to where the literary agent sat.

Marcus might have been grieved by the death of his client and friend, but it didn't appear that his sadness had affected his appetite as he tucked into the sandwich in front of him. He glanced up when Faith approached.

Maisie let out a small bark in greeting.

"Do you mind if I join the two of you?" Faith asked.

"Not at all. We would welcome the company," Marcus said. "As news of Vanessa's death has spread through the convention, I seem to have become a sort of pariah. I imagine the others don't know what to say to me, and they probably find it easier to avoid me altogether."

"I'm sorry. That can't be easy," Faith said. "I have to confess that I do have an ulterior motive for seeking your company, however."

"Oh?" Marcus broke off a bit of bacon from the sandwich and held it out to Maisie, who sniffed it before gulping it down in a most unladylike fashion. He dabbed at her muzzle with a napkin, then turned to Faith. "What might that motive be?"

Faith plunged ahead. "Do you happen to have Vanessa's copy of *The Damsel's Fate*?" She watched Marcus's expression closely. It wasn't that she expected him to lie, but she wanted to know if the question came as a surprise.

His usually rosy cheeks grew even ruddier. "No. Why do you ask?"

"We can't find the book," Faith admitted, "and I was wondering if Vanessa had given it to you."

"Maybe you should check with Meredith," Marcus said, reaching for his cup of coffee and taking a long sip. "If Vanessa entrusted it to anyone, it would have been her."

"I just checked with Meredith, and she says she doesn't have it either," Faith said. "She suggested that someone could have killed Vanessa in order to steal it."

Marcus appeared startled.

"It is a valuable book," Faith said, "and I know Vanessa kept it in her room."

"Yes, and I would bet that other people have their eye on it."

"Really? Like who?"

"Deb Fremont," Marcus answered. "She has an online store that sells antique and rare books."

Faith tried to hide her surprise. The fact that Deb already had a market and an outlet to sell *The Damsel's Fate* put a whole new spin on the situation. Combined with the fact that Deb might have been stalking Vanessa, it was starting to look bad for the woman.

"Deb approached me the other night and peppered me with questions about the book," Marcus continued. "She's extremely interested in it, and she wants to buy it."

"Is that what you were talking about at the unveiling ceremony?" Faith asked.

"Yes. I told her it was up to Vanessa, of course, but she kept asking me questions," Marcus replied. "Then I let Vanessa know about Deb's interest and recommended that she leave it locked up after the event ended."

"How did Vanessa react?"

"She was furious that Deb was inquiring about her book," Marcus said. "And obviously she refused to follow my advice for its security."

"Do you know if she had the book insured?" Faith asked.

"Although Vanessa was my client and friend, I didn't want to pry into her personal matters. I don't even know if she had life insurance." Marcus took another sip of his coffee, then leaned back in his chair. "As a matter of fact, I'd be surprised if she did. Vanessa didn't have any family to leave her money to."

Faith thought she had never heard anything so sad in her life. At a glance, Vanessa seemed to have it all—beauty, plenty of money, and professional success. But what did any of those things matter without anyone to share them with? What was the point without real, human connection? And now that Vanessa was gone, only her fans—people who didn't even know her—would miss her because they wouldn't get any more books.

Faith felt overwhelmingly grateful for all the people in her life she cared about and who cared about her as well. She resolved to give each of the dear women at the book club meeting an extra hug tonight.

"Thanks for your time. I'll let you finish your meal," Faith said, pushing back her chair.

"I've got to keep up my strength since I'll be spending the rest of the day notifying her publishing contacts about her death. It's so tragic." Marcus sighed, then returned his attention to his plate.

Faith left him alone with his thoughts. As she exited the room, she almost ran into Deb, who was clearly in a great hurry to get somewhere. Faith paused and watched the woman's rapidly retreating form.

Vanessa had been convinced that Deb was stalking her. And Deb knew the value of *The Damsel's Fate* and how casually Vanessa had treated its security. Faith didn't want to believe it, but she couldn't help but wonder if Deb had stolen the book and killed Vanessa.

A chill crept up her spine. Was she staring at a murderer?

12

On her way to the library, Faith saw Wolfe passing through the lobby, and she filled him in on what Meredith and Marcus had told her about the missing book.

"It's time to notify the police about the possible theft," Wolfe said.

Even though Faith knew the police should get involved, there was still a sinking feeling in the pit of her stomach. She hated to think that someone might have stooped low enough to disrespect the priceless volume by stealing it and possibly killing its owner.

"I'll call Garris and let you know when I hear something," Wolfe said as he stepped into the elevator.

When Faith reached the library, Bernadette was standing by the door.

"I'm sorry to keep you waiting," Faith said as she unlocked the door and invited her inside.

"Oh, don't worry about it," Bernadette said. "I just got here. Can you point me to the romance novels?"

Faith led her to the section. "How are you feeling after your accident?"

"Much better," Bernadette said. "I spent a long time resting and catching up on my reading yesterday." She grinned. "That's why I'm searching for another novel."

"Can I help you find a specific book?" Faith asked.

"I'm just browsing. I like to scan until something catches my eye."

Faith smiled. "Well, please let me know if you need anything." She retreated to her desk to make some more headway on her to-do list.

Another guest entered the library, and Faith helped the woman locate the reference materials she sought.

When Faith returned to her desk, Bernadette walked over with a book. "I'd like to borrow this one, please."

"Of course." Faith checked the book out and handed it back.

"Thank you." Bernadette paused and lowered her voice. "Do you have a minute?"

"Sure." Faith motioned to her guest chair. "What's on your mind?"

Bernadette sat down and placed the book on her lap. "I was wondering about Vanessa's death. At first I thought it was only a nasty rumor."

"I wish it were," Faith said.

"I heard that you found her body."

Faith nodded.

"How did she fall down the stairs? Was it an accident? Or . . . ?" Bernadette's voice trailed off.

"The police are considering the death suspicious."

Bernadette shook her head. "I hate to say it, but I'm not exactly surprised. Vanessa was the kind of person who made a lot of enemies. It was difficult just being on the panel with her. I can't imagine working with her all the time."

"She seemed rather demanding," Faith agreed. "But it sounds like the people who worked with her the closest got along with her well."

"Maybe so, but I still don't know how her assistant put up with her day in and day out. I would have quit within the first week."

"I'm sure that it was a job that wouldn't have appealed to everyone," Faith said. "But Meredith seems to have been able to deal with whatever Vanessa threw at her."

"That may be true, but Vanessa angered plenty of other people here," Bernadette pointed out.

"Who are you referring to?" Faith asked.

"Carol Lynn accused her of stealing her idea in front of everyone," Bernadette reminded her. "And Theresa was furious that Vanessa blamed her for Carol Lynn's presence and for the phony newsletter."

"You're right. Beverly seemed quite angry with Vanessa too."

"Yes, she was," Bernadette said quietly. She gazed down at the book on her lap.

"Is something wrong?" Faith asked.

Bernadette stared at Faith for a moment before responding. "I hate to say this about my adviser, but I saw Beverly leave Vanessa's room the morning Vanessa died."

"What?" Faith's mind spun. What had Beverly been doing in Vanessa's room? Had they argued again? Had Beverly stolen *The Damsel's Fate* and then murdered Vanessa? She shivered.

"My suite is close to Vanessa's," Bernadette continued. "When I was walking out of mine, I saw Vanessa standing in her doorway and seeing Beverly out."

"Did you talk to Beverly about it?"

"No. She didn't notice me, and I didn't feel right about telling her I saw her. I didn't want her to feel like I was spying on her or suspected her of anything." Bernadette raised her chin. "I know what you're thinking, but Beverly would never steal a book, and she would definitely not kill someone."

Faith wasn't so sure about Beverly's innocence on either count. Even though Bernadette sounded confident, Faith had to keep in mind that Beverly was the young woman's academic adviser. Was Bernadette's judgment clouded by her relationship with Beverly?

"Have you told any of this to the police?" Faith asked.

"I haven't talked to the police at all," Bernadette said. "Why would they want to speak with me?"

"They're questioning everybody who is attending the retreat," Faith replied. "I'm sure they're planning to get around to you eventually. When they do, you should tell them about this."

"I wouldn't want to get anyone in trouble, especially not Beverly," Bernadette said.

"Even so, I think it would be better if you told them what you saw," Faith said.

"If they ask me directly if I saw Beverly leaving Vanessa's room, I'll tell them," Bernadette answered. "But if they don't ask, I'm not going to bring it up."

Faith wondered why Bernadette was unwilling to volunteer the information. It wasn't as if she'd seen anything exactly incriminating. She'd only witnessed Beverly leaving Vanessa's room. Perhaps Bernadette harbored a seed of doubt about Beverly's innocence after all.

"Besides, I also saw Theresa going into Vanessa's room," Bernadette went on.

"You did? When?"

"It was the night of the unveiling," Bernadette said. "I was returning to my room when I saw the two of them enter Vanessa's suite."

Faith recalled how Theresa had fled the library when Vanessa entered, so why would Theresa go to Vanessa's suite? Not to mention how Theresa had blamed Vanessa for pushing her off the stage after the panel discussion, and Vanessa had threatened to sue Theresa over the fake newsletter. Faith couldn't imagine either of them wanting to be near the other.

Had Theresa made up some kind of excuse to get inside Vanessa's room so she could steal her book out of revenge?

Faith suddenly realized something. "You witnessed Beverly leave Vanessa's room the morning she died?"

"That's right," Bernadette said. "Why?"

"Because you may have been one of the last people to see Vanessa alive. Do you remember exactly what time it was?"

"It was a few minutes before I went on my ill-fated bike ride," Bernadette said. "I didn't check my watch because there was nowhere I needed to be until after the group returned from the trip to Orchard House."

"Did you see Vanessa again yesterday morning?" Faith asked. "I mean, after you saw Beverly leave Vanessa's room?"

"No, I didn't. I went to borrow a bicycle not long after I saw

Beverly walk out of Vanessa's room," Bernadette said. "I have no idea what happened to either of them after that."

"I'm sure the police will appreciate anything you can tell them about Vanessa's movements yesterday morning," Faith said.

The other patron approached, interrupting them. "Can I borrow these?"

"Of course," Faith said, then turned to Bernadette. "Please excuse me for a minute."

"I need to get going anyway." Bernadette raised the book. "I have some reading to do." She stood and strode out of the room.

As Faith assisted the other guest and sent her on her way, she considered what Bernadette had told her.

Even though Bernadette's room was near Vanessa's, it seemed strange that Bernadette had happened to see two people who had grudges against Vanessa enter and leave the author's room. What were the odds?

Something else occurred to her. Had Bernadette made the stories up for some reason?

No, Faith couldn't see her making up a story to cast her beloved adviser in a bad light.

So assuming Bernadette was telling the truth, why had Beverly and Theresa gone into Vanessa's suite in the first place? Had one of them stolen Vanessa's copy of *The Damsel's Fate*? It didn't seem to be a secret that Vanessa had kept the valuable book in her room.

But why would Vanessa let them inside? If the other women's accusations were true, Vanessa had stolen Beverly's property and pushed Theresa off the stage.

Faith was also surprised at Bernadette's reluctance to speak with the police. She could understand why the young writer would not want to cast suspicion on her adviser, but what if she had something to hide? If that was the case, her story had probably been made up. After all, she was a writer.

Faith's phone rang, jolting her out of her thoughts.

It was Chief Garris. "Wolfe reported the theft of *The Damsel's Fate*, and I have some questions for you," he said. "Would you meet me in the upstairs den in half an hour so we can go over them?"

Faith agreed, then disconnected.

Before meeting the chief, she made a detour to the kitchen to talk to Brooke. It was between meals, so she hoped her friend would have a few minutes to spare.

"I wondered how long it would be before you stopped by," Brooke said. "How are you holding up?"

"You mean, how am I holding up after finding our guest of honor dead yesterday?" Faith asked.

"I mean, I'm guessing it's not exactly easy. That must have been horrible."

"It really was," Faith said, shivering. "I couldn't believe what I was seeing."

"Have some coffee. It'll warm you up." Brooke filled a large mug with steaming, fragrant coffee, then handed it to Faith.

"Thank you." Faith sat down at the small table in the back corner of the room and took a tentative sip. Her stomach rumbled, reminding her that she'd missed lunch. "Oh, sorry," she said with a grin.

"You forgot to eat, didn't you?" Brooke walked to an industrial refrigerator and peered inside. "How about some lasagna? You can't go wrong with carbs and cheese."

"That sounds perfect," Faith said.

Brooke placed a generous piece of lasagna on a plate and slid it into the microwave. When it was done, she set the plate and a fork down in front of Faith.

"Thanks again." Faith took a bite. For a few seconds, she was able to forget all about murders and thefts as she simply enjoyed the delicious food.

Brooke sat down at the table next to her. "Marlene was in here earlier, and she told me that the police had decided to use the upstairs den as a base for their investigation today. She didn't seem exactly happy about it."

"That's no surprise. Marlene's never thrilled when something happens that requires a police presence at the manor."

"With Vanessa's death and the police investigation, I was wondering if the ball would be canceled," Brooke continued. "But Marlene told me it's still on the schedule."

Faith had almost forgotten about the costume ball. It was meant to be one of the highlights of the conference, and she knew the guests were anxiously awaiting it.

The manor staff had been planning the decorations for weeks. The Great Hall Gallery had been festooned with urns and vases awaiting bouquets of flowers. Carefully polished silver candlesticks sat upon the sideboards in readiness, and every crystal in the enormous chandelier had been thoroughly cleaned.

"I'm glad," Faith said. "The guests would be very disappointed if the ball was canceled."

"That was how I felt too." Brooke moved to a large wooden board draped with a tea towel. She pulled back the fabric to reveal discs of dough a few inches across.

"What are you making?" Faith asked.

"I found a new recipe for English muffins, and I thought I'd test it." Brooke pulled an electric griddle from a large cabinet and plugged it into an outlet. "Would you like to try one?"

Faith drained the last of her coffee. "After eating your delicious lasagna, I really should say no. But I'd love one."

Brooke smiled as she began to set the muffins on the griddle. "There's nothing like comfort food on a tough day."

"I need all the comfort I can get," Faith said. "The murder was bad enough, but now Vanessa's copy of *The Damsel's Fate* is missing."

Brooke glanced up, her eyes wide. "Missing?" she echoed.

Faith sighed. "Yes. Marlene and I searched for it in her suite, and

I've asked everyone she might have given it to for safekeeping. But the book is nowhere to be found."

"Do you think the missing book has something to do with Vanessa's death?" Brooke asked as she flipped the muffins over.

"I'm on my way to talk to Chief Garris. He wants to ask me some questions about the book. He might be thinking that same thing."

"Good luck," Brooke said. She slid two muffins onto a plate. "Let's see how these came out."

Faith accepted one and took a bite. It was light and chewy and melted in her mouth. "It's delicious."

Brooke sampled her own muffin. "Why don't you take some of them to your meeting?"

Faith nodded. "That's a great idea. But are you sure you can spare them? I don't want to leave you in the lurch if you'd planned them for something else."

"These were just a trial run, but I think they turned out well enough to share," Brooke said. "Let me know what the chief has to say about them."

"I will." Faith pushed back her chair and stood.

"Don't forget we have a book club meeting tonight," Brooke said as she packed the muffins into a bakery box. "We have a lot to talk about."

The Candle House Book Club enjoyed discussing books, but the meetings were also a forum for bringing up whatever else was going on in their lives. Tonight Vanessa's murder was sure to be a topic of discussion.

"I wouldn't miss it," Faith said. She accepted the bakery box and napkins that Brooke held out to her. "Thanks for the food. And thank you for listening. I'm really lucky to have a friend like you."

"My pleasure. Now get going before the muffins get cold."

When Faith entered the den on the second floor, she found Chief Garris and Officer Laddy sitting at the table.

Faith hadn't realized Laddy would be in the meeting, so she was glad that Brooke had sent plenty of English muffins. She raised the bakery box for them to see. "I thought you might need some refreshments."

"We were just talking about getting something to eat. You must be a mind reader," Chief Garris said. "What do you have?"

Faith placed the box in the center of the table and removed the lid. "Homemade English muffins. Brooke used a new recipe, so she'd love to know what you think." She passed them the napkins.

Garris and Laddy eagerly helped themselves. When they polished off their first ones in record time and went back for more, Faith concluded with a smile that the recipe was a success.

Chief Garris popped the last bite into his mouth and wiped his fingers on a napkin. "Delicious. My compliments to the chef."

"Mine too," Laddy said, reaching for a third muffin.

"Faith, I need to ask you about the book Wolfe reported stolen." The chief picked up a notepad and a pen from the table in front of him.

"I'm ready to help in any way I can," Faith said. "What do you need to know?"

His expression grew serious. "Wolfe told me the book is extremely valuable. Is it valuable enough to cause someone to kill?"

"Yes, I would say so," Faith answered. "The book is very rare. We have a companion copy to it here in our collection, and the manor has a substantial insurance policy on it."

Laddy whistled. "It definitely sounds like something worth stealing."

"But that doesn't necessarily mean someone murdered Ms. Langston to get his or her hands on it," the chief pointed out.

"I really hope not," Faith said. "But the book is missing, and the timing is suspicious to me."

"Wolfe said you were the one to raise the alarm about the missing book," Garris said. "Is that correct?"

"Actually, Dr. Beverly Johnson asked me about it," Faith answered. "I was so rattled after finding Vanessa's body that I didn't give the book a thought until she brought it up."

"So when did you decide to search for it?"

"It was after Beverly asked to see it. She said Vanessa had offered to let her borrow it," Faith answered. "When Marlene and I went to retrieve it from Vanessa's room, it was nowhere to be found."

"Why did Dr. Johnson want to see the book?" Laddy asked.

"It has significant historical value, and Beverly wanted to reference it for her research," Faith said. "She's writing a book about Louisa May Alcott and thought it would be of use."

"Is there any reason to think that Ms. Langston would have had the book with her when she died?" Garris asked. "If it was worth that much money, would she have been carrying it around? Wouldn't she lock it up somewhere?"

"Vanessa seemed surprisingly cavalier about the book's value," Faith answered. "I really can't say what she was likely to have done since I didn't know her well, but I do know that she ignored her agent's suggestion and Wolfe's offers to keep it in either the manor safe or the glass display case while it was here."

"Did you check to see if someone was keeping the book for Ms. Langston?" the chief asked.

"Yes, I talked to her agent and her assistant, but they both said she hadn't given the book to them. I was told she wanted to have easy access to it at all times for a series she was writing, and she thought everyone else was being paranoid about the book's safety."

"Do you have a reason to suspect that either the agent or the assistant could be lying?" Garris asked.

"No, at least not anything definite," Faith said. She felt uneasy at the thought of telling unfounded tales, but at least one serious crime had been committed. Now was not the time to worry about her own discomfort. She needed to give the police any information as well as any suspicions she had.

"Is there anything else you want to tell me?" The chief raised his eyebrows. "It sounds like you know something I should hear."

Faith wondered if she had stuck her nose in where it didn't belong, but Garris didn't seem angry. He only seemed curious. "It's about the argument between Vanessa and Beverly that I mentioned to you. It happened not long before the fall must have occurred, and it sounded very heated."

Garris flipped through his notepad. "Are you referring to Dr. Johnson's accusation that Ms. Langston stole her laptop and her research?"

"Yes, that's the one."

"You think it could be a strong motive for Dr. Johnson to either steal from Ms. Langston or to orchestrate her murder," the chief said thoughtfully. "Noted. Is there anything else on your mind?"

"Marcus said that Vanessa rubbed most people the wrong way and that as far as he knew she didn't have any family," Faith said. "He didn't even know if she had a life insurance policy, since she wouldn't have had anyone to leave it to. I don't know what that means for your investigation, though."

"That might have some bearing on the direction we take. What else do you have?"

Faith hesitated, then decided to tell the chief what she'd heard from Bernadette. It felt a little like betraying the woman's confidence, but Faith had to be sure the chief knew everything about the case. "Bernadette Varney's room is near Vanessa's, and she told me she saw Theresa enter Vanessa's room and Beverly leave it."

"When was that?" he asked.

"Bernadette said Theresa was in the room the night of the unveiling and Beverly the morning Vanessa died."

"Thanks for your help." Garris met her eyes. "You will be sure to let me know if you find out something else, won't you?"

"Absolutely," Faith said. "Please let me know if you hear anything about the book."

"We'll be sure to tell you right away if it turns up," the chief said. Then his expression grew serious. "Be careful. There's still a murderer on the loose."

13

Faith went in search of Meredith to let her know the police were looking into the missing book.

She checked the main areas of the manor, including the dining room and the salon, but to no avail. She even asked several of the guests if they had happened to see Meredith, but none of them had.

Faith decided to stop by Meredith's room. What better place to work in privacy than behind the locked door of her own suite?

As Faith approached the room, she heard a strange noise. She paused, thinking it was a conversation between two people. Maybe she was in luck and Meredith was indeed inside. She knocked on the door.

A moment later, she heard rustling from within.

Meredith opened the door halfway. "Oh, it's you. Is there something you need?"

"I wanted to give you an update on *The Damsel's Fate*," Faith answered.

"Please come in." Meredith stepped back and opened the door wider.

The first thing Faith noticed when she entered the suite was a large birdcage in the corner. A green-and-orange parrot sat on a perch beside it. Had Meredith been talking to her bird when Faith arrived?

"I didn't realize your parrot was here," Faith remarked. "You said that Vanessa wouldn't allow you to bring him."

"You're right," Meredith said. "Since Vanessa forbade it, I had to smuggle Ferdinand into my room, and I couldn't tell anyone about it."

"Hello!" Ferdinand squawked.

Faith chuckled and approached him. "Hello to you too."

Ferdinand blinked at her slowly. The bird lifted one foot and inspected his claws. Then he tipped his head forward and raised his feathers in Faith's direction.

"Well, isn't he a sweetie," Faith remarked.

"Pretty bird," Ferdinand said.

"Yes, you are." Faith reached out and gently stroked his soft head. Ferdinand leaned into her finger.

She didn't think that Watson would be particularly happy if she added a parrot to their home, but she had to admit the idea was tempting at the moment. The last parrot she and Watson had encountered had not been nearly as well-mannered as this one.

Faith turned to Meredith. "I can see why you didn't want to leave him at home."

"I had to bring him," Meredith said. "My neighbor who usually watches him for me is on vacation. I couldn't just leave him home by himself to starve or to die of loneliness." She leaned forward and clucked her tongue at Ferdinand. "Could I, pretty boy?"

The parrot hopped to the other side of the perch and reached his beak toward her.

Meredith gave him a little kiss.

"Couldn't you have told Vanessa what had happened with your pet sitter?" Faith asked. "It wasn't as though Ferdinand would have been any trouble if you left him here in your room."

Meredith shook her head. "Vanessa feels strongly about all pets, so I ended up checking into the manor ahead of her and sneaking Ferdinand into my room."

"Did Vanessa ever find out you brought him?" Faith asked.

"No. Ferdinand was a good boy and stayed quiet. He never even squawked." Meredith held out her forearm, and Ferdinand hopped onto it in one smooth motion.

The brightly colored bird climbed carefully up Meredith's arm and sat on her shoulder. He reached his beak toward her hair and took a strand of it in his mouth.

Faith realized the bird was grooming Meredith in a gesture of affection.

Meredith reached up and stroked Ferdinand's chest. "So, you wanted to give me an update on *The Damsel's Fate*."

"Unfortunately, no one has been able to locate the book," Faith admitted.

"That's terrible. What happens now?"

"The book has been reported missing," Faith answered. "The police are treating the theft as a possible motive for her murder."

"Just what I thought." Meredith frowned. "It's so tragic that Vanessa might have been killed over a book."

Faith nodded. Since she was here, she thought she'd ask Meredith some questions. Maybe the assistant would be able to give her a clue as to who was responsible. "Do you have any idea who could have done this?"

"As you already know, the book was rare and extremely valuable," Meredith said. "Many people at this retreat would have been interested in owning it."

"But who would have gone to extreme lengths to get it?" Faith asked.

"That's a good question," Meredith said. "The first person who comes to my mind is Deb."

"Why do you say that?" Faith asked.

"Because she was stalking Vanessa, and she desperately wanted her copy of *The Damsel's Fate*."

Faith had heard as much from Marcus. She had to admit that it didn't look good for Deb. She seemed obsessed with Vanessa and with her book. Had Deb taken her fixation too far?

"Thanks for letting me know about the book, but I really should get back to work. I have a lot of people to notify and arrangements to make," Meredith said as she walked to the door and opened it. "And I expect the police are going to ask me some more questions."

Faith followed. "I'm sure they'll be in touch."

"Pretty bird," Ferdinand said, bobbing his head.

As Faith walked down the corridor, she considered the missing volume. There was still no telling if it had been stolen at the time of the murder. Maybe it had actually been taken from Vanessa's room.

If that was the case, then who would have been in a better position to steal the book than Beverly or Theresa? According to Bernadette, they had both been in Vanessa's room. It would have been easy for one of them to slip the book into a bag when Vanessa wasn't paying attention.

As much as she didn't like to think so, Beverly and Theresa seemed like the strongest suspects in the theft. Which meant they might also be the strongest suspects in the murder.

14

When Faith returned to the library and settled at her desk, Watson hopped onto her lap. He sniffed her hands even more thoroughly than usual, and she wondered if he could tell she had been patting Ferdinand's head.

When he was satisfied, he jumped down, then sauntered out the door. Evidently, he had some feline adventure ahead of him.

Patrons came and went, most of them with questions for Faith about what had happened to Vanessa. A few of them even had photos of the crime scene tape stretched across the corridor on their cell phones.

Faith wondered if the images would be making their way around social media. She shuddered at the thought.

Even though she found it entirely distasteful, she imagined that Vanessa would have approved. The woman had seemed to be interested in self-promotion and drama in all its forms. In some small way, Vanessa might have been delighted to know that she was still making headlines. For all Faith knew, the author's book sales would spike once word got out that she had been killed.

The entire afternoon passed rather quickly, and soon it was time to close the library for the day. Faith checked out a few books and ushered the last patrons out the door.

As she shelved some stray books, Watson strolled into the room.

"And what have you been up to, Rumpy?"

The cat turned his head, ignoring her. Then he sat down and began grooming his tail.

She still had some time before the book club meeting, so she decided to get her thoughts on paper. Maybe writing them down would help her organize them. She took a seat at her desk and found a notebook and a pen.

There were two lines of investigation to pursue. One was Vanessa's murder, and the other was the disappearance of *The Damsel's Fate*. Not for the first time, Faith wondered if the two events were somehow connected.

She also wondered why Vanessa had been on her way to the basement in the first place. She must have been headed down that staircase. Otherwise, she wouldn't have tripped on the fishing line. But the guests at the manor had no need for service areas.

Besides, Vanessa seemed like the sort of person who valued being seen. Using the back stairs didn't seem to be her way. Maybe there was a reason she didn't wish to be seen entering the lower level. Could she have been secretly meeting someone?

Faith wrote the questions in her notebook, then set her pen down and scanned her notes. She still had too many questions and no answers. Each question just led to more questions.

Like those surrounding *The Damsel's Fate*. Where could the book have gone? And was it really possible that Vanessa had not left her estate to anyone? If so, what would happen to her copy of the book—if they ever found it?

If someone had stolen the volume, would the thief try to sell it? Would it matter whether or not they could prove provenance? After all, it wasn't as though the book needed authenticating like a painting by a Dutch master would. The thief could claim to have bought it at a garage sale or a secondhand shop. As long as the book could be proven a first edition—which would be revealed by a simple glance at the copyright page—that was all anyone needed to know before purchasing it.

Once again, Faith felt irritation rising in her chest at Vanessa for being so irresponsible with such a valuable volume. As a librarian and an avid booklover, she could not condone Vanessa's attitude, even if it hadn't led to a missing treasure of a book.

The list of suspects for the theft could easily include every single person attending the conference. They were fans of Louisa May Alcott's work, and they could easily have researched exactly how valuable Vanessa's copy of *The Damsel's Fate* actually was.

She considered the possibility of someone taking the book from Vanessa's room. The volume wasn't very large, and there could have been any number of ways for someone to distract Vanessa while absconding with her possession.

Meredith and Marcus worked closely with Vanessa, so they would have had plenty of opportunities to enter her suite. Either one of them could have knocked on Vanessa's door under false pretenses in order to take the book.

Theresa had admitted to Faith that she could hardly stand to be in the same room with Vanessa, yet Bernadette had seen Theresa leaving the author's room. Why? Had Theresa been angry enough at Vanessa to steal the book in order to get back at the author?

And what about Beverly? Of all the people involved in the Pickwick Club, no one would have been more aware of the financial and literary value of Louisa May Alcott's work. Not to mention that Beverly had accused Vanessa of taking her research. Had Beverly stolen from Vanessa to even the score?

There were far too many suspects, and she had no idea how to narrow the field. Faith decided she would pose her questions to the book club. Whenever she found herself searching for answers, she turned to them for guidance. Eileen, Midge, and Brooke were sure to help her see things in a different light.

She tucked her notebook and the Alcott resource materials to return to Eileen in her bag, then slung the strap over her shoulder. "Come on, Watson. We have just enough time for dinner before the book club meeting. What do you say?"

Watson perked up his ears at the mention of food, then sprinted to the door.

Faith followed Watson into the Candle House Library. She was glad to be spending the evening in such good company.

Midge, Eileen, and Brooke were already gathered in the comfortable chairs in front of the fireplace. Atticus, Midge's Chihuahua, sat in her lap. He was wearing his Doggles, specialty glasses for his failing eyesight.

Eileen was busy with her latest knitting project. At first glance it appeared to be a bright-blue baby sweater. But then her aunt handed it to Midge, who placed it across the tiny dog's back to measure it, and Faith realized it was intended for Atticus.

Watson jumped onto the back of a chair opposite Midge and narrowed his eyes.

Faith couldn't tell if he was displeased with the dog's presence or the sweater's. Some guests at the manor had recently knitted sweaters for him out of Angora rabbit wool, and Watson had made his feelings about them perfectly clear by destroying one of them.

Atticus stood up in Midge's lap and furiously wagged his tail in greeting. The little dog never seemed to give up hope that someday he'd become Watson's friend.

Watson flattened his ears and settled down with his back to Atticus.

Faith set the stack of resource materials on the end table next to Eileen. "Thanks for letting me borrow these."

"You're more than welcome," Eileen said.

Faith paused to give Atticus a pat on the head before settling into the chair Watson had chosen.

"Brooke was just filling us in on all the terrible things that have been going on at the manor." Eileen gave Faith a stern look. "I would have thought my niece would tell me herself."

"I'm so sorry," Faith said. "I haven't had a chance to call with all the craziness."

"I suppose I can forgive you," Eileen said, her face softening into a smile. "But be sure to keep me posted on any developments."

"I will," Faith promised.

"Is it true that the police think Vanessa Langston was murdered?" Midge said. She returned the sweater to Eileen.

"I'm afraid so," Faith replied.

"I'm so glad you weren't hurt," Brooke said.

Faith shivered. "I don't think I'll ever be able to use the back stairs again without seeing Vanessa's body crumpled at the bottom of them."

Eileen rested a reassuring hand on Faith's arm. "Is there anything we can do?" she asked.

"Just being here with all of you is a great deal of help," Faith said. "It's good to get away for a little while and to talk about books."

The other three women nodded and pulled their copies of *Little Women* out of their bags.

Watson, apparently faced with the realization that there would be no treats until after the meeting, leaped to the floor and strode off.

After a lively discussion of the lives of the March sisters and their beloved Marmee, conversation once again turned to Vanessa and the murder.

"As much as I have always enjoyed Vanessa's books, I'm not very enthusiastic about her continuing the Little Women series," Midge said. "I never like it when one author picks up where another one left off. You can always tell that it's someone else telling the story, and that makes it a different story to me."

"I don't know," Brooke said. "I think it can be fun to see where someone else's imagination will take a familiar set of characters. How do you feel about it, Eileen?"

"It depends on the quality of the work and whether or not the author is able to maintain a similar tone to the originals. It's not easy to do."

"Do you think that Vanessa's work will successfully imitate Louisa May Alcott's?" Brooke asked.

"It doesn't sound like it will." Eileen set the book down and resumed her knitting.

"Why not?" Brooke asked.

"I hate to spread gossip, especially considering Vanessa is no longer able to defend herself," Eileen said. "But I heard through the grapevine that the publisher had to delay publication of her manuscript."

"They delayed it?" Midge leaned forward in her chair. "Why would they do that?"

"If the manuscript doesn't meet the publisher's expectations, they can reject it and ask for significant changes," Eileen said. "That can cause a serious delay in the publishing schedule if the author requires a lot more time to fix it."

"Is it unusual to delay manuscripts?" Midge asked.

"It happens, but I believe it's unusual for an author as experienced as Vanessa. Actually, I've never heard of this happening to a seasoned professional."

"Why would they have rejected the manuscript?" Brooke asked.

"It can be several different things," Eileen said. "It could be the quality of the writing, the themes explored, or even the length of the manuscript. Maybe she missed her deadline and threw off the publisher's schedule. A book as highly anticipated as Vanessa's would have had an enormous impact on a publishing house if it was greatly overdue."

"How did you hear that there was a problem with Vanessa's book?" Faith asked.

Faith never failed to be astonished by her aunt's broad network of connections. Not only did she know most everyone in Lighthouse Bay, but she was involved in several librarian organizations at both the state and national levels. She also occasionally wrote book reviews for a number of different online and print publications, often receiving advance reading copies of books long before they were available to the general public.

"One of the editors of a review site I contribute to mentioned it in an e-mail," Eileen responded. "She said she received a message from Vanessa's publishing house notifying her of the delay. She wanted me to know because we had discussed that I would review it when it came out."

"I wonder if Vanessa managed to make the revisions before she died," Faith said.

"I haven't heard anything about the changes," Eileen replied.

"Meredith Harris or Marcus Tripp might know whether she had finished them," Faith said. "As her assistant and her literary agent, they would see how her work was progressing."

"Do you think it could have had anything to do with her murder?" Midge said.

"It's a possibility," Faith admitted. How would problems with the manuscript provide a motive for Vanessa's murder? She wondered who could have stood to gain if the Littlest Women series was not published.

"Since that's the sort of information that the police are not likely privy to, I think Chief Garris should be informed about it," Eileen said. "I expect he'll want to check it out as a possible motive."

"What will happen to the book series if Vanessa didn't make the revisions?" Brooke said. "Will they cancel it?"

"I think that's likely," Eileen said. "A big part of the draw was Vanessa's name on the cover."

"Would it really make that much of a difference?" Midge asked.

Eileen nodded. "The publisher knows that readers don't trust many authors to continue classic series correctly. They probably don't have anyone else on standby to do it now. And they were likely banking on crossover from fans of her other books buying the new ones as well. If readers love one set of books from an author, they're usually willing to try anything else that same author writes."

"I completely agree," Brooke said. "I love Vanessa's historical novels, and I was looking forward to this new series because she was the one who wrote them. I'm not sure I would have paid much attention if it had been someone else."

"That's the impression I've gotten from patrons here at the Candle House Library too," Eileen said. "There were a lot more people referring to it as Vanessa Langston's next novel rather than the new Littlest Women book. I just can't see how the publisher would manage to make it worth their while if she couldn't be listed as the author."

Yet something else to mention to Chief Garris, Faith thought. What reason could someone have had to keep the publishing house from releasing the Littlest Women series? Who would benefit from such a thing? Could there be a rival publisher who wanted to launch a new series based on Louisa May Alcott's work?

But was it really likely that a publishing house might be involved with something criminal? Faith shook her head. She was letting her imagination run away with her. Besides, as far as she knew, there were no representatives of any publishing house staying at the manor.

More than one publisher could release a continuation of the Little Women series anyway. After all, there were many books on the market at any given time with surprisingly similar themes. How often had someone written the further adventures of Sherlock Holmes? And what about the numerous retellings of fairy tales?

No, she couldn't imagine that a rival publishing house was involved. But she still had no idea who could have wanted Vanessa out of the way.

"Eileen, have you heard any rumors about Vanessa having personal problems with anyone?" Faith asked.

Eileen paused in her knitting. "Yes, now that you mention it, I remember reading posts from someone who claimed that Vanessa had stolen her idea for the Littlest Women series."

"Was it Carol Lynn Dodge, by chance?"

"That's her," Eileen said. "How did you know?"

"She's attending the retreat, and she made the same claim during a panel discussion Vanessa was participating in," Faith explained. "Her accusation created quite a stir."

"I'm not surprised," Eileen said. "Carol Lynn tried to organize a boycott of Vanessa's books, and she even made threatening comments to Vanessa."

"Threatening comments?" Faith repeated. She couldn't hide her shock. Carol Lynn had been outspoken when she accused Vanessa of plagiarism, but she hadn't seemed like a violent person. Was it possible that she'd taken her threats further?

"What happened?" Brooke asked.

"The debate became so heated and ugly that the entire thread was deleted by the administrator," Eileen answered.

"Carol Lynn claimed to have proof that Vanessa stole her idea," Faith said.

"She made the same statement online," Eileen commented. "She said that she posted Littlest Women stories in online forums a long time before Vanessa announced that she was writing the new series."

Brooke raised her eyebrows. "Is it possible that Vanessa really stole Carol Lynn's idea?"

"I don't know." Eileen sighed. "And now that Vanessa is gone, we might never find out."

"Are there any other writers who would have a motive?" Midge asked.

"Bernadette Varney isn't exactly a fan of Vanessa's," Eileen answered.

"After the way Vanessa treated Bernadette at the panel discussion, I can understand why," Faith said.

"When Bernadette came here to the library searching for Louisa May Alcott materials, I got the impression it was mainly to avoid Vanessa," Eileen said.

"What do you mean?" Brooke asked.

"Bernadette mentioned that Vanessa had approached her at the manor with some questions about the original books because Bernadette did her thesis on Alcott," Eileen explained. "Bernadette said she wouldn't have minded an in-depth conversation with Vanessa, but her questions were so rudimentary that Bernadette wondered if Vanessa had even read the books. Bernadette believed the project was beyond Vanessa's abilities."

"Did Bernadette say anything else about the new series?" Faith persisted.

Eileen nodded. "She told me that she hoped it would never see the light of day."

"She seems like such a mild-mannered person," Faith said. "I'm surprised that she had such a strong opinion about Vanessa's books. Did she sound angry?"

"Yes, she did," Eileen said. "She was vehement that a continuation of the series was wrong."

"So there are two writers who had been angry with Vanessa," Midge summarized. "I'm sure there are other people who felt the same way about her."

"I encountered her only once, but she got on my nerves." Brooke's usually sunny face clouded over. "No one has ever complained so much about the food at the manor."

"Did she complain to you directly?" Faith asked. Usually the guests did not have a lot of interaction with Brooke personally. She was generally far too busy in the kitchen.

"No. She complained to Theresa, who passed on her concerns to Marlene. I'm sure you can imagine how that conversation went," Brooke huffed. "I went home and told Diva and Bling about it. They were so depressed that they spent the rest of the night hiding out at the bottom of their tank."

Faith stifled a smile. Brooke often projected her emotions onto her pet angelfish without realizing it.

"I wouldn't take her comments to heart," Faith said. "During her short time at the manor, Vanessa criticized everything from her suite to the library."

Brooke gasped. "How could anyone with even a slight appreciation of books be unhappy with the library?"

Faith gave her friend a grateful smile. She'd felt the same way.

"Is there any reason the police can be certain that Vanessa was the one who was supposed to trip down the stairs?" Midge asked thoughtfully. "How could the killer be sure someone else wouldn't pass through there instead?"

"I asked Chief Garris the same thing when Vanessa's body was first discovered," Faith responded. "He said that he couldn't be sure that she was the intended victim, but they were going to use that assumption as a place to start."

"You don't suppose it was the work of a prankster who didn't think about how severe the consequences would be, do you?" Brooke asked. "Could someone else at the manor be in danger?"

"I'm sure no one else is in danger," Midge said, reaching out and giving Brooke's hand a firm squeeze. "Right, Faith?"

"If anyone else was in danger, Chief Garris would have stationed several officers at the manor to keep us safe," Faith said with far more confidence than she actually felt.

After all, *The Maiden's Plight* was still in the library, which meant that if anyone was still in danger, it was her.

15

When Faith and Watson arrived at the manor the next morning, they saw Chief Garris and Officer Rooney ushering Deb down the hallway.

Faith was shocked. Had Deb been arrested? And if so, was it for murder or theft? Or both?

Even though her little dog, Rapunzel, was nowhere to be seen, Watson took off in the opposite direction.

When Deb noticed Faith, she broke away from the police and rushed toward her.

Garris clenched his jaw. "Not so fast, Ms. Fremont," he said, his voice ringing with authority.

Deb glanced over her shoulder at the chief, then turned to Faith. "I need you to do me an enormous favor." She reached out and grasped Faith's arm.

Trying not to show alarm at a potential murderer's touch, Faith asked, "What do you need?"

"I want you to look after Rapunzel for me while I'm gone," Deb said, releasing Faith's arm. "I'm sure I'll be back soon, but I can't stand the thought of her being trapped in my room with nothing to eat and no one to walk her or keep her company."

"I'll be happy to help," Faith said. "Don't worry about Rapunzel. I'll take good care of her."

"Thank you," Deb said, wiping the tears from her eyes.

"Officer Rooney, will you escort Ms. Fremont to the squad car?" Chief Garris asked. "I need to have a word with Miss Newberry."

Officer Rooney nodded, then took Deb's arm and led her down the hallway and toward the door.

Just before they were out of sight, Deb cast Faith a terrified glance over her shoulder.

When they were gone, Faith asked the chief, "Did you get my message last night?" After the book club meeting, she had left a voice mail to tell him about Vanessa's revisions and the delay in the first book of the Littlest Women series.

He nodded.

"So what are you arresting Deb Fremont for?"

"We're not arresting her yet," Garris clarified. "We're taking her in for questioning for the murder of Ms. Langston and also the theft of *The Damsel's Fate*."

"Why is she a suspect?"

"You told me yourself that Ms. Langston considered Ms. Fremont a stalker," Garris answered. "And she has an online store that sells antique and rare books. She already has a way to sell the stolen copy of the book."

"I know, but many people attending the retreat could sell that book even without an online store," Faith argued. "Not to mention there are several booksellers offering their wares here. Why single out Deb?"

"We also had a witness report that Ms. Fremont was the last one to board the bus for the field trip that morning."

That was new information. Faith's mind spun.

Before she could ask anything else, the chief said, "If we're lucky, we might be able to close the entire case soon. But I need to go find out for sure." He tipped his hat and hurried after Officer Rooney and his prime suspect.

Even if Deb was guilty, Faith had promised her she'd take care of her dog. She went downstairs to ask Marlene for the key to Deb's suite.

She walked by the offices that used to be the servants' quarters. Space was tighter in the basement than it was on the other floors of the manor, but it still felt far from claustrophobic.

Faith stopped at the door marked *Assistant Manager* and knocked. "Come in," Marlene barked.

Faith walked inside cautiously. From Marlene's gruffer-than-usual response, she was almost afraid of what she might find.

Marlene sat at her desk surrounded by piles of paper and folders. She glanced up from her work. "What is it? I need to finish this report today."

"It will only take a minute," Faith said. "I need to borrow the key to Deb Fremont's suite."

"You know I can't give you the keys to guest rooms," Marlene said, then picked up one of the papers.

"I know, but this is a special circumstance. Chief Garris and Officer Rooney just took Deb to the station for questioning."

Marlene set the paper down and stared at her. "Questioning?"

"Apparently Deb is a suspect in Vanessa's murder and the theft of her book," Faith explained. "Deb's dog is in her suite, and she asked me to take care of her."

Marlene picked up her key ring, removed a key, and handed it to Faith. "She's in the Emily Dickinson Suite."

"Thank you. I'll bring it right back."

"See that you do." Marlene refocused on her task—a clear dismissal.

Faith left the office and closed the door behind her. On the second floor, she rushed to the Emily Dickinson Suite and went inside.

Rapunzel barked from her kennel.

Faith located Rapunzel's leash and opened the kennel door.

The little dog bounded out and danced around, obviously excited to be released. She finally calmed down enough for Faith to snap the leash onto her collar.

Faith locked the door, then led the dog downstairs and outside.

Rapunzel scampered around the lawn, stopping every few feet to sniff bits of greenery emerging from the cold, damp earth.

Watson appeared around the edge of a holly bush as if to remind

Faith that it was he, not some interloping dog, who deserved her devotion.

Rapunzel caught sight of him and yanked on her leash, barking and growling. Faith was grateful the dog was too small to drag her.

Watson sat down, absently inspecting one of his paws as if to display how little concern he had for Rapunzel's clear threats.

Faith wondered what would become of Rapunzel if Deb did not come back soon. While she had promised to take care of the dog, she didn't see how Rapunzel could stay with her and Watson at the cottage. There would be no peace if she brought the dog home.

She decided the best thing to do was to take Rapunzel to the kennels. That way she wouldn't have to bother Marlene for the key to the Emily Dickinson Suite several times a day to walk her. The little dog would be treated well and be less lonely—Faith imagined she would miss her mistress—but it wasn't a permanent solution.

On the other hand, she didn't need a permanent solution right now. She would wait and see how things played out with Deb before making any decisions about the dog.

Theresa rounded a forsythia hedge that was just beginning to show traces of brilliant yellow. "Isn't that Deb Fremont's dog?" she asked as she joined Faith.

"Yes, this is Rapunzel," Faith replied. "I'm keeping an eye on her for a while."

"I thought I saw Deb headed away from the manor in the back of a police car." Theresa raised her eyebrows. "So the police have solved the murder?"

"I can't speak for the police," Faith said carefully. "All I can say is that Deb asked me to watch Rapunzel for her."

"You don't have to say anything. Rumors have been flying through the conference about all sorts of people." Theresa dropped her voice to a conspiratorial whisper. "Including Deb."

"You can't always trust rumors."

"I was surprised when I heard she was stalking Vanessa, but it looks like there must have been some truth to the rumors," Theresa went on as if she hadn't heard. "Mind you, my guess was Beverly."

"Why did you think Beverly was involved?" Faith asked, even though she had her own suspicions about the professor.

"She wanted the copy of *The Damsel's Fate*," Theresa said. "I heard her say so myself."

"I think she had that in common with everyone at the conference," Faith said. "Mr. Jaxon offered to buy it for the manor's library, but that doesn't make him a suspect."

"I'm sure everyone would love to possess the book," Theresa conceded. "But Beverly is the one I distinctly heard telling Bernadette Varney that she would kill to own it."

"When did you hear that conversation?" Faith asked.

"At the unveiling ceremony," Theresa said. "When I learned that Vanessa had died, I thought it must have been an accident. But when I found out the book was missing, my first thought was that Beverly had killed her for it." She checked her watch. "Oh, I have to run. There's a new session starting."

Faith frowned as she watched Theresa go. Was she right? Had Beverly decided that stealing Vanessa's book was suitable retaliation for her stolen research? Had she concluded that the easiest way to get the book was to get rid of its current owner?

More questions popped into Faith's mind. Why had Theresa seemed so eager to cast suspicion on Beverly? Did she have something of her own to hide?

16

The Great Hall Gallery glowed with soft, flickering candlelight. Enchanting classical music drifted through the air. As Faith gazed around, she imagined the room was filled with characters from Louisa May Alcott's books. All around her, women dressed in hoopskirts clustered in small groups and chatted with one another. The air rippled as dozens upon dozens of silk fans fluttered back and forth with flicks of delicately gloved hands.

Faith smoothed the front of the emerald-green satin skirt of her own costume. While she enjoyed the occasional pleasure of dressing up, she was grateful that such a dress was not something she was expected to wear every day. It had taken a long time to get ready.

She wondered if Louisa May Alcott had longed to go about in pants as Faith usually did. She thought of Beverly's remarks that Louisa had been an unhappy woman who had struggled to find her place in a restrictive world.

"You look far too serious for a woman who is sure to be the belle of the ball," Wolfe said as he stepped up behind her.

She turned to thank him for the compliment, and her voice caught in her throat. She was not sure she would have recognized him if he hadn't spoken. He had darkened his hair to a rich shade of brown. His upper lip and chin were covered by a false mustache and beard. He even appeared to have gained a few inches around his waist.

Faith stifled a laugh and motioned to his top hat. "Who are you supposed to be?"

Wolfe placed a hand on his chest as if in mock surprise. He spoke again, this time with a thick German accent. "Do you not recognize me? Am I not the very image of Professor Bhaer?" He sketched a slight bow.

Faith smiled. "Of course you are. I was just speaking about you the other day. I am so glad you were able to find time to attend the ball."

"You surprise me. I am not accustomed to being the topic of conversation. Should I be alarmed?"

"Certainly not. I believe I was expressing a preference for your company to that of Laurie's," Faith said. "I do think that Jo chose wisely in the end. She and Laurie were quite ill-suited, I think."

"I'm gratified to hear you say it," Wolfe said. "Will you do me the honor of this dance?" He held out his arm.

Faith nodded and took his arm.

Wolfe led her through the crowded room to a space at the edge of the dance floor. A small orchestra was positioned on the far side of the room. The lights from the chandelier glinted off their instruments.

Wolfe was an excellent dancer. As they turned in time to the music, Faith felt all the concerns of the past few days melting away.

Now and again she caught glimpses of the guests she recognized. Theresa, Marcus, Carol Lynn, and Beverly were all dressed in appropriate period costumes.

She managed a small wave at Bernadette as Wolfe gracefully spun her around. She was glad the writer had recovered from her bike accident and was able to attend the grand event.

When the music stopped, Faith was grateful that her costume included a fan. All the dancing in close quarters had caused the room to grow quite warm.

"Would you care for a glass of punch?" Wolfe said. "I know I could do with one."

"That sounds lovely," Faith said. "Thank you so much for offering."

"I'll be back in a moment."

Faith watched his retreating form as he slipped through the crowd to the refreshments table. She let her gaze drift around the room as she admired the period costumes of the other guests. Most of the women wore hoopskirts, and many of them were dressed as Jo March. Quite a few must have been wearing wigs, because she didn't remember so many attendees with long brown hair.

Even Meredith had covered her short hair with a long brown wig. She was almost unrecognizable without her glasses and wearing a costume complete with lace gloves and ornate jewelry. In fact, Faith probably wouldn't have known it was her if it hadn't been for her parrot, Ferdinand, sitting on her shoulder and plucking at her wig.

Marcus stood beside Meredith. He wore an opulent midnight-blue velvet jacket and shiny shoes. His dog, Maisie, was dressed for the occasion as well. She was dressed in a tiny blue velvet dress of her own. A wide satin sash was tied around her, and the bow sat jauntily in the middle of her back.

Maisie and Ferdinand were not the only pets in attendance. Dogs and cats sporting costumes and jeweled collars wandered around the room. Faith observed two dogs approaching each other, one lowering its head as if to bow to the other. It was almost as if the animals were having a ball of their own.

Brooke walked up to Faith. "I saw you dancing with Wolfe. You make a very attractive couple."

"Wolfe and I are just friends," Faith reminded her.

"Whatever you say," Brooke teased. "Any news about the investigations?"

Faith pulled Brooke into a secluded alcove so no one would be able to eavesdrop. She quickly filled her in on the police taking Deb in for questioning and what Theresa had told her about Beverly.

"I wonder if Deb will be arrested," Brooke said. "And what about Beverly?"

"I don't know. It seems—"

"Excuse me," Marlene interrupted as she strode over to them. "Brooke, you're needed at the refreshments table."

Brooke nodded and hurried away.

"I'm glad we didn't have to cancel the ball," Faith said to Marlene. "It seems like the guests are enjoying themselves."

"I suppose," Marlene conceded as she scanned the room. "But I'd rather not see all these animals roaming around."

Faith followed Marlene's gaze and noticed Marcus carrying his little dog.

As Faith watched, Marcus flagged down Wolfe when he walked away from the refreshments table with two glasses of punch. They talked for a moment.

Then Wolfe made his way to Faith and handed her a glass of punch.

"Thank you," Faith said. The punch was a deep rosy color. When she took a sip, she found it was the perfect balance of sweetness and tartness—beautifully refreshing.

Wolfe turned to Marlene. "Thank you for all your hard work in organizing the ball. It's a wonderful event."

"I'm glad you're satisfied with it," Marlene said with a small smile.

"I wanted to let both of you know there's going to be a pause in the dancing," Wolfe said.

"Has something happened?" Faith asked. While she didn't want anything to spoil the evening, she wouldn't mind resting another moment or two before returning to the dance floor.

"Mr. Tripp has an announcement he'd like to share with the guests," Wolfe replied. "He asked me if he could do so before the evening winds down and the guests start to leave."

"What kind of announcement?" Marlene asked.

"He didn't say." Wolfe motioned to Marcus as he walked to the corner of the room where the orchestra was set up. "I think we're about to find out."

Marcus spoke briefly with one of the musicians, a tall man holding a violin. The man gestured at a microphone.

Marcus plucked the microphone from its stand. "Excuse me, ladies and gentlemen. May I have your attention, please?"

The chattering among the guests tapered off.

"I have some exciting news to share with you," Marcus said. "First of all, thank you for coming out this evening despite the recent tragedy in our midst. I know Vanessa would have wanted everyone to continue to enjoy the retreat even though she could not be with us."

Faith thought she saw a dubious expression on a few faces.

"Vanessa loved the opportunity to gather with fellow readers at wonderful events like this one," Marcus said. "Which brings me to a bit of good news that I just couldn't wait to share with all of you."

Marcus gave a broad smile, then said, "I wanted you to be among the first to know that despite Vanessa's untimely death, her publisher has decided to continue with their plans to release a continuation of the Littlest Women series."

The crowd murmured in surprise, and skirts rustled as attendees faced their neighbors to gauge their reactions.

Marcus tapped on the microphone to regain everyone's attention. "Vanessa left several manuscripts for the series mostly completed. With such a volume of work at their disposal, the publishing house has decided to release one new Littlest Women book each year for the next four years."

Cheers broke out in the room. Many guests were smiling, and others engaged in animated conversations.

"I can see that you are as pleased about the news as I am," Marcus said. "Be sure to look for the first book in the Littlest Women series in bookstores soon. Or let the publisher know how much you value the contribution Vanessa made to the literary world by preordering your copy."

"I can't believe it," Faith murmured to Wolfe. "Eileen was just telling the book club that she had heard rumors that Vanessa's first Littlest Women book wouldn't be ready on time. I can't imagine how it ended up being finished."

"That does seem to be a bit of a trick," Wolfe said. "Are you sure the rumors that your aunt heard were correct?"

"No," Faith admitted. "She learned about problems with the manuscript in one of her book review forums. But there's always talk about controversial books, especially those that pick up where a classic series left off. Still, I wonder how they're going to pull it off."

"It sounds as though they have a lot of material to work with," Wolfe said. "That's not unheard of, is it? Authors frequently work on books way in advance."

"That could be the reason why Vanessa was searching for additional source material to inspire her work," Faith said. "Maybe she wasn't having trouble with the first book in the series but rather one several books into it."

"We should do our part and preorder a copy for the library," Wolfe suggested.

"I'll be sure to add it to my list of purchases," Faith promised.

As Faith scanned the room, she was pleased to see so many excited guests. Obviously, many of the attendees were delighted by the big news.

Then she noticed a trio who stood out because they appeared visibly upset. Bernadette, Beverly, and Carol Lynn huddled close together. They were in deep discussion.

The three women had major issues with Vanessa and the series, so they were certainly distressed about the announcement that it would continue without her.

Faith almost gasped aloud when an idea hit her. Perhaps the police had taken the wrong person into questioning. Maybe they should be searching for more than one suspect for the crimes.

What if these three had conspired to murder Vanessa and steal her copy of *The Damsel's Fate*?

17

The next morning, Faith and Watson left the cottage early so they could stop in at the kennels to check on Rapunzel before opening the library. Faith found herself hoping that Deb had been released from the station and had already picked up her dog.

When Faith and Watson arrived, Annie Jennings, the young kennel attendant, walked out of the office and greeted them. "You're here bright and early," she said with a smile. It was hard to be glum around Annie, with her sparkling eyes, freckled nose, and tender care of the animals in her charge. "What's up?"

"I wanted to check on Rapunzel before work if she's still here."

"Yes, Rapunzel's here. Follow me."

Faith's heart sank. Deb must still be at the station. She would have definitely claimed her dog if she'd been able. Had the chief arrested her after all?

As Annie led Faith inside, she said, "Rapunzel doesn't seem to be adapting very well to her mistress's absence."

"What do you mean?"

"When I came in earlier, the attendant on the night shift said that Rapunzel spent much of last night whining," Annie replied, then stopped in front of Rapunzel's kennel.

The dog was curled up in the far corner.

"I think Rapunzel wore herself out," Annie remarked. "A few minutes ago, I took her outside to play with the other dogs, but she wouldn't engage any of them."

Faith's heart broke for the poor dog who was clearly bereft without her owner.

"It might help if Rapunzel had an article of her mistress's clothing,"

Annie suggested. "The scent could be a comfort to the dog."

"That's a good idea," Faith said. She checked her watch. "I have enough time to retrieve something from Deb's suite. Can I take Rapunzel with me?"

"Sure, a walk and some fresh air will do her good." Annie grabbed a leash hanging on a peg nearby, then opened the kennel door. She removed a treat from her pocket and coaxed Rapunzel over to her. She snapped the leash on the dog's collar and handed it to Faith.

At first, Rapunzel seemed uninterested in going anywhere. But then Watson appeared in the doorway, and the dog started barking and tugging on her leash in an attempt to get closer to the cat.

"That's the liveliest I've seen her," Annie commented.

"I guess she just needed a little incentive," Faith said. "See you later."

As soon as Faith and Rapunzel began walking, Watson bounded off, and Faith didn't see him again until she and Rapunzel reached the manor. He stood at the door, waiting for them. He bolted inside the building as soon as she opened the door, careful to stay out of Rapunzel's reach.

She'd already returned Deb's room key to Marlene yesterday. She sighed at the thought of asking Marlene if she could borrow it again.

As Faith trudged downstairs to the assistant manager's office, Marlene came bustling down the hallway toward them.

Marlene stopped and frowned at Rapunzel trotting next to Faith. "I thought you took that dog to the kennels."

"I did, but she's having some separation anxiety," Faith said. "Annie suggested retrieving an article of Deb's clothing to help calm the dog down."

Marlene sniffed. "I'll never understand why people have pets. They're such a nuisance."

Not for the first time, Faith wondered why Marlene worked at a pet-friendly establishment, but she kept the question to herself as usual. "May I borrow the key to Deb's suite again?"

Marlene gave Faith the key from the ring at her waist, then continued down the hall.

Faith and Rapunzel went up to the second floor. Faith opened the door of the Emily Dickinson Suite, then closed it behind her.

Rapunzel seemed overjoyed to be in familiar surroundings. When Faith let go of the leash, the dog raced around the room, sniffing and yipping as though she expected to find Deb there somewhere.

Faith didn't want to think about how Rapunzel would react when she discovered Deb was still nowhere in sight.

She scanned the room for an article of Deb's clothing to take to the kennels. It was tidy and most things seemed to be put away, but Faith spotted a scarf on the back of one of the chairs. She was glad that she wouldn't have to go digging through another guest's belongings.

When Faith retrieved the scarf, she noticed a small tote bag on the floor. Inside, she could see a brightly colored ball and a rawhide bone. She decided it wouldn't hurt to take some of the dog's favorite toys too, so she reached into the bag and pulled out a stuffed octopus. She called Rapunzel and dropped the stuffed octopus to the floor.

The little dog immediately pounced on it and began chewing on one of its legs, her tail whipping back and forth.

As she straightened, something on the nearby desk caught her attention. Two laptops rested side by side.

Faith opened the lid of the closest laptop and pressed the power button. The screen flickered on, and Deb's name appeared.

Faith lowered the lid and reached for the second computer. She opened it with a sinking feeling. Beverly's name appeared on the screen.

She closed the computer and glanced at the file folders and notebooks stacked on the desk. Since Deb had Beverly's computer, then the rest of the materials must be her research.

To make sure, she reached for the closest file folder and flipped it open. It was filled with photocopies of letters written in old-fashioned script as well as newspaper clippings and photographs of the interior of Orchard House.

Then Faith sifted through a stack of several more folders and found a few notebooks at the bottom. She skimmed the pages of one of the notebooks.

There was no doubt the folders and notebooks belonged to Beverly.

While Faith set the notebook aside, another thought occurred to her. If Deb had stolen the research, had she stolen Vanessa's copy of *The Damsel's Fate* too? Did Garris have the right person after all?

She would have to do a thorough search of the room.

With Rapunzel happily distracted by her toy, Faith was able to make quick work of her search. Within a few minutes, she was certain *The Damsel's Fate* was not there.

Eager to leave, she gathered up all the folders, the laptop, and the notebooks and slipped them into the tote bag that held Rapunzel's dog toys. She carefully slung the bag over her shoulder, then bent down to pick up Rapunzel and her toy octopus. There was no time to waste convincing Rapunzel to leave the room. She wanted to return Beverly's research as soon as possible.

As Faith locked the door behind her, she couldn't help but wonder how she could have been so wrong about Deb's character.

If she was capable of stealing the research, was she capable of an even worse crime?

Breakfast was being served in the dining room, so that was the first place Faith looked for Beverly. When Faith poked her head inside, she saw Beverly getting up from her table, so she waited at the door for her with Rapunzel.

A few moments later, Beverly appeared.

"I'm so glad I caught you," Faith said. She removed the laptop, file folders, and notebooks from the tote bag.

Beverly's eyes widened. "My laptop and research! Where did you find them?" she asked, taking her belongings and inspecting the contents of the top folder.

"They were in Deb Fremont's room," Faith responded. "I found them on her desk just now when I was searching for some items for her dog, Rapunzel." She motioned to the dog, who had plopped down at her feet.

"What could she have possibly wanted with my research?" Beverly asked, sounding surprised. "She's not a scholar, and I don't know why she'd have had a personal grudge against me. I hardly know the woman."

"I have no idea," Faith admitted. "But I'm going to inform the police."

"Thank you. I can't tell you how grateful I am that you found these for me." Beverly clutched her items to her chest. "Now I'll be able to get back to work on my book, but this time I won't leave my belongings unattended for even a moment."

Beverly's words gave Faith an idea. "How long were you away from your research?"

"Less than ten minutes," Beverly said. "Why do you ask?"

"I'm just thinking about timelines and possibilities," Faith answered. "You said that you had set up your work in one of the small studies on the far side of the manor?"

"That's right. I chose it specifically because it was off the beaten track and well away from all the commotion of the conference," Beverly said. She regarded Faith. "Is that important for some reason?"

"It might be," Faith said. "I think I have more to share with the police than I thought."

"I'd better run. I need to check through all my notes and make sure everything is here. Thanks again." Beverly hurried down the hall.

Faith glanced down at Rapunzel, who was still sitting on the floor. "How would you like to go see Deb? I think we may have some good news for her after all."

18

It was only a short drive from the manor to the Lighthouse Bay police station. On the way, Faith called Laura. Fortunately, she was available to open the library and keep an eye on it until Faith got there.

After Faith parked, she lifted Rapunzel from the back seat and carried the dog up the sidewalk. The police station was located inside a clapboard Cape Cod, and it blended in almost seamlessly with the surrounding architecture. The only dead giveaways were the antennae on the roof and the police cruisers parked behind it.

When she walked inside, she was greeted by Daphne Kerrigan. The receptionist smiled and gestured at Rapunzel. "Who's your friend?"

"This is Rapunzel," Faith replied. "She belongs to Deb Fremont."

At the sound of her name, the little dog wagged her tail.

"Is that why you're here?" Daphne asked. "To see Ms. Fremont?"

"Actually, I'd like to talk to Chief Garris. Is he available?"

"Let me check." Daphne picked up the phone and made a quick call. She hung up and adjusted her glasses. "He'll be free in a few minutes. Come on back."

Faith followed Daphne past several desks and into a small room.

"The chief will be with you shortly," Daphne said, then walked out and closed the door behind her.

Faith sat down at the small table in the center of the room. She put Rapunzel on her lap and scratched the dog's ears. The small dog was trembling, but Faith couldn't tell if it was from the cool temperature or fear of an unfamiliar place. She idly wondered if Watson would ever forgive her for leaving him behind while she took a dog to town, especially one who so clearly disliked cats.

A few minutes later, the chief walked in and closed the door. He sat down across from her and set a file folder on the table in front of him. "I understand you have something on your mind."

"I think Deb Fremont has an alibi for the time of the murder," Faith said without preamble.

"Ms. Fremont claims that she didn't kill Ms. Langston or steal her copy of *The Damsel's Fate*," Garris said. "If you have some evidence that will help to exonerate her, I'd like to hear it."

"I believe it will clear her on the current charges." Faith paused. "Unfortunately, her alibi is that she was busy committing another crime."

The chief removed a notepad and a pen from his shirt pocket. "What other crime?"

"Stealing Beverly's research and her laptop," Faith replied.

Garris flipped open his notepad and started scribbling in it. "How do you know?"

"I just discovered all of Beverly's possessions in Deb's room," Faith answered.

The chief stopped taking notes and stared at Faith. "Why were you in Ms. Fremont's room?"

She glanced down at Rapunzel sitting on her lap. "This is her dog. She has separation anxiety, and one of the kennel attendants suggested getting an article of clothing from Deb's room to comfort the dog."

"I see."

"I didn't find *The Damsel's Fate* anywhere in the room," Faith continued.

"She could have hidden it somewhere else at the manor," Garris reasoned. "Officer Rooney is on her way to the manor to search Ms. Fremont's room. If the book is in there, she'll find it."

"Is the fact that Deb sells rare books on the Internet enough of a reason to hold her if she has an alibi for the time of the murder?" Faith asked. "After all, how can you be sure exactly when the book was stolen?"

"You're right about that," the chief conceded. "We decided to charge Ms. Fremont with the theft as well, but we're holding her on the strength of the evidence about the murder."

"What evidence?" Faith asked.

Garris frowned. "We found fishing line in her purse."

Faith sat back in her seat, stunned.

The chief scraped back his chair and stood up. He opened the door, then called out to Officer Laddy and asked him to escort Deb to the room.

Within moments, Officer Laddy and a haggard-looking Deb darkened the doorway.

Rapunzel leaped from Faith's lap and ran to her mistress. She stood up on her hind legs, yipping and wagging her tail with excitement.

Deb picked up the little dog and made cooing noises at her.

The officer closed the door and left.

"Ms. Fremont, please take a seat," Garris said. "Some new information has just come to light, and I have some additional questions for you."

Deb nodded and sat in the chair next to Faith's, cuddling Rapunzel close.

"I understand why you weren't more forthcoming about your movements during the time of Ms. Langston's murder." The chief gestured to Faith. "Would you like to take it from here?"

"I think you have an alibi for the time of the murder," Faith told Deb. "I'm not sure that it gets you entirely out of hot water, but at least you wouldn't be facing a murder charge."

Deb's eyes widened, and she pulled Rapunzel closer to her chest. "What do you mean?"

"Rapunzel has been absolutely beside herself without you, and one of the kennel attendants thought an article of your clothing might comfort her," Faith explained. "So I was in your room this morning searching for something to take to the kennels."

Deb hugged Rapunzel even more tightly.

"While I was in there, I happened to see Beverly's laptop on your desk along with all her research folders and notebooks."

"Did you steal those things?" the chief asked Deb.

She hung her head and slowly nodded. When she gazed pleadingly at the chief, her eyes were filled with tears. "I did take the professor's research. And her laptop too."

"Why?" Garris asked. "Are they valuable to you?"

Deb shook her head, and a tear fell onto Rapunzel's head. She wiped it off with her hand. "I took Beverly's research to get back at her for all the nasty things she said about Vanessa Langston's upcoming book series."

"When did that happen?" Faith asked. "I don't remember anything like that at the panel discussion the other day."

Deb took a ragged breath. "I overheard Beverly talking about Vanessa's work with Bernadette Varney. Beverly said that the book she was writing was sure to stir up controversy about Vanessa's new books."

"Overhearing that conversation made you decide to steal Dr. Johnson's research?" the chief asked.

"Beverly claimed that Vanessa was a hack riding on the coattails of a far more successful author," Deb replied, her voice becoming shrill. She appeared agitated. "She said she intended to mention that to news outlets whenever any of them contacted her for an interview."

Faith couldn't help but wonder if Deb was indeed a bit unbalanced. Vanessa had accused her of being a stalker, and Deb had stolen Beverly's research because of a few comments the professor had made.

"So you slipped into the room and took Dr. Johnson's belongings on the morning of the Orchard House field trip?" Garris asked.

Deb nodded.

"Tell me exactly what happened," the chief said.

"I took Rapunzel out to the kennels at the manor so I could attend the field trip," Deb said. "After I dropped her off, I came back into the manor through a door at the rear of the building. As I entered, I spotted Beverly leaving a room ahead of me. I waited for her to turn the corner, and then I walked into the room she had just left."

"And you found her work all set up and left unattended?" Faith asked.

Deb nodded. "That's when I decided to steal it. It seemed to me that she shouldn't be allowed to finish her own book if she planned to promote it by ruining Vanessa's reputation. I gathered it all up as quickly as I could. Luckily I was wearing a coat and was able to conceal Beverly's laptop and all the research underneath it until I could get back to my room."

"This is all very interesting and does clear up one mystery at the manor, but how does it help with an alibi for Ms. Fremont?" Garris asked.

"Because of the timing," Faith said. "Even though a witness claimed that Deb was the last one on the bus for the field trip, she still managed to make it before it left for Orchard House."

"How does that give her an alibi?" the chief asked.

"I don't believe Deb could possibly have had time to steal the professor's research, stash it in her room, and then go to the other side of the manor to string the fishing line across the top of the stairs," Faith answered. "She wouldn't have been able to get on the bus before it left."

"We don't know when the fishing line was stretched across the stairs," Garris pointed out.

"It must have been done right before Vanessa fell down the stairs," Faith said. "Marlene told me that she had gone down those stairs shortly before. In fact, we were both a bit shaken up to think that either one of us could have been in Vanessa's place."

"And you think that proves Ms. Fremont could not have been the one to cause Ms. Langston's fall?" the chief asked.

Faith nodded.

"Do animal owners have to sign their pets in at the kennels?" Garris inquired.

"Yes, the kennel employees sign pets in and out," Faith answered.

The chief leaned back in his chair. "So there should be a record of the time Ms. Fremont was there with her dog?"

"When you check the records, I'm sure you'll discover that Deb couldn't be responsible for both the theft of Beverly's research and the murder," Faith said.

Deb spoke up. "I wasn't the last one to board the bus."

Garris opened the file folder and paged through the case notes and witness statements until he found what he was searching for. "Carol Lynn Dodge told Officer Tobin that you dashed onto the bus at the very last minute and that you sat in one of the only remaining seats."

Deb sniffed. "She ought to know. Carol Lynn followed me onto the bus. The driver closed the door behind her and said that we both needed to take our seats right away if the bus was going to get to Orchard House on time."

"Why would Ms. Dodge lie about being the last person to board the bus?" the chief said.

"Maybe she was stringing the fishing line at the top of the stairs," Deb suggested. "She's the one who picked a fight with Vanessa in front of a roomful of people."

"Several other witnesses mentioned Ms. Dodge causing a scene." Garris turned to Faith. "You told me about it too. Refresh my memory about what she had to say."

"She claimed Vanessa had gotten the idea for the Littlest Women series from some stories she posted online," Faith said.

Deb snorted. "As if a writer as accomplished and talented as Vanessa would need to stoop to stealing ideas from someone else."

Rapunzel grunted as if to add her own two cents to the conversation.

"Do you know if there was any truth to her claims?" the chief asked Faith.

"I only know what other people at the retreat told me," Faith said. "Theresa Collins claimed that Carol Lynn could prove that she had posted fan fiction in forums well before Vanessa announced she was writing the new series."

"That does give us another line of inquiry to follow if Ms. Fremont could not have committed the murder." Garris stood and closed his notepad, then addressed Deb. "We have to keep you here while Officer Rooney searches your room and we test out Faith's timing theory. And you're still going to have to answer to the charge of stealing Dr. Johnson's research."

"I understand. It was a spur-of-the-moment decision, but it was still wrong." Deb clutched Rapunzel. "Do you have to take my dog back to the kennels, or could she stay here with me while you verify my alibi?"

Rapunzel seemed to sense Deb's distress, and she began to whine.

"I have a soft spot for dogs myself," the chief said. "If you can promise that she won't be any trouble, I think we can allow Rapunzel to stay with you while you wait."

"Thank you," Deb said.

Garris opened the door and called for Officer Laddy to usher Deb and Rapunzel out of the room.

Once they were gone, the chief said to Faith, "Thanks for coming in and bringing this to my attention."

"I'm glad I could be of assistance," Faith said. "But giving Deb an alibi doesn't help solve the murder, does it?"

"I'm afraid not," Garris said. "Do me a favor and be careful. I don't have any reason to suspect anyone else is in any danger, but I would feel better knowing you weren't taking any unnecessary risks."

Faith felt her heart speed up. If she had been fooled by Deb's character, could she be tricked just as easily by the real killer?

19

Faith drove back to the manor with a heavy heart. She had always thought she had good instincts, but the truth was she felt rattled and adrift.

There was only one thing to do. She parked in her usual spot and made her way to the library. She always felt everything would be all right when she surrounded herself with books, and there was no better place in the world to do that than Castleton Manor.

Laura was studying a textbook when Faith walked in.

"Thanks for covering for me," Faith told her. "I'm sorry I've been gone so long."

"I don't mind. I've enjoyed it." Laura gestured to the textbook in front of her. "And I even had some time to tackle my homework." In addition to her duties at the manor, Laura was taking classes in library science. Wolfe had worked out a deal with her. He paid for each class in which she earned an A. Faith admired his generosity.

Faith glanced around. The library was indeed quiet. It was empty of patrons except for Beverly, who was camped out at the large table with her research materials and her laptop.

Laura followed Faith's gaze. "Dr. Johnson is thrilled that you found her things. She's been here since a few minutes after you left. Said she has a lot of catching up to do."

"I'm glad," Faith said. She scanned the rest of the room but didn't see her cat. "Have you seen Watson lately?"

"No, he hasn't been in here this morning." Laura checked the clock. "Oh, I should get going." She packed up her books and notebooks, slid them into her backpack, and left.

Faith decided to check on the professor. Watson was probably wandering the manor as he so often did. He'd make an appearance when he was good and ready.

Beverly glanced up and smiled as Faith approached.

Faith thought Beverly looked ten years younger than she had when she first told Faith that her research had been taken.

"I cannot thank you enough for finding all this for me," she said. "I will be sure to mention you in the acknowledgments page."

Faith felt touched. "You don't have to do that."

Beverly waved off her protest. "Nonsense. You've made the book possible again. You belong there."

"Well, I've never been mentioned in a book before," she said, taking a seat opposite Beverly.

"I'm surprised it hasn't happened already. Librarians are so often a resource for writers, and you must have helped a number of them."

Faith shrugged. "That may be so, but you're the first to offer it to me."

"It would be my pleasure. Tell me, what did Deb Fremont give as a reason for taking my research and laptop in the first place?" Beverly asked, leaning forward eagerly.

"She overheard you casting aspersions on Vanessa's new series," Faith answered. "When she saw your belongings unattended, she decided to keep you from completing your own book to get back at you for the things you said."

Beverly raised her eyebrows. "Is that all? I had no idea Vanessa inspired such devotion from her readers. Deb risked being arrested to punish me for a passing comment? I can hardly believe it."

"Deb said she was also upset to hear that you were planning to use any controversy raised by your criticism of Vanessa's new series to create interest in your own book. Is that true?" Once again, Faith considered how Beverly could profit from Vanessa's death and the theft of her book. What could cause more sensational headlines than a high-stakes robbery and a murder?

"My publisher planned to time the release of my book to coincide with Vanessa's Littlest Women launch," Beverly said. "They thought highlighting its controversial nature and message would provide great publicity for the book."

"Would that work?" Faith asked, surprised.

"My publicist has scheduled a long list of radio and television appearances right around the launch date," Beverly said. "They're facing some tough times financially, and they need my book to sell far better than average to help keep them afloat."

"So your publisher has a lot riding on this book coming in on time?" Faith asked.

"Not just my publisher," Beverly said. "Vanessa's publisher is probably in the same boat with her work."

"How would Vanessa's publisher benefit?" Faith asked.

"Controversy is good for everyone," Beverly said. "It has a way of bolstering sales of all books connected to it. I would expect to see an uptick in preorders for Vanessa's book, my own, and even the original Louisa May Alcott books. People will want to read everything for themselves and decide how they feel about it."

"So any press is good press?" Faith asked.

The professor nodded.

Beverly's reasons seemed sound, but Faith was still unsure that there wasn't more to the scholar than research and academia. There was no love lost between her and Vanessa, and she certainly had good reason to want to get her hands on the copy of *The Damsel's Fate*. It would certainly prove a good source for her research, and she might even want to keep it afterward, knowing how Louisa May Alcott had felt about it.

Faith knew that many of the thefts of famous works of art were carried out for collectors who had no wish to profit financially from the crime. They simply wanted to possess a rare and beautiful object for their private enjoyment. Why should book collectors be any different?

"It's not easy to make a living in publishing," Beverly continued. "I always counsel my graduate students to think about the ways their degrees can help them rather than just being a source of crippling debt."

"Is that a common problem?" Faith asked.

Beverly nodded. "So many of my students have a romantic notion about the world, and it gets them into a great deal of trouble, at least as far as money is concerned."

"Bernadette Varney was one of your students, wasn't she?" Faith said.

"Yes, and she was the most talented and hardworking student I ever had the pleasure to advise. Now, if she had been the one who took on the project of continuing the Little Women series, I might be more supportive of its merits."

"Why didn't the publishing house choose someone like Bernadette to write the books?" Faith asked. "Isn't she more qualified because of her expertise?"

"That's not really how the publishing world works. Vanessa Langston is a household name, and Bernadette Varney isn't. They're going to go with a name that people know because it's more likely to sell well." Beverly sighed. "Bernadette is a wonderful writer, and she deserves to be more recognized for her work."

"Was Bernadette one of the students who racked up debt for her degree, but it didn't pan out?" Faith said.

"Unfortunately, yes," Beverly answered. "Bernadette is working in a coffee shop to pay off her student loans."

Faith had to wonder if Bernadette could possibly have been involved in the theft of *The Damsel's Fate*. She definitely knew its value, and she might have academic contacts who would be interested in purchasing the valuable book from her. Bernadette could pay off her loans and probably have plenty of money left over.

"If the publishing business is such a challenge, why do you

think that anybody wants to do it?" Faith asked.

Beverly shrugged and pointed at the paper spread out in front of her. "Given what I know about Louisa May Alcott and my own personal experience working on this book, I would say it isn't a question of what writers want. By all accounts, people who write books simply can't seem to help themselves."

Faith glanced around the library. She was overwhelmed with gratitude for all the work and countless hours so many writers had put into the books contained on the shelves. So many of them had never become famous. Most of them never earned a living from their art. But all the people who read their stories were enriched by their efforts.

"You make a very convincing argument," Faith said. "Do you plan to press charges against Deb for stealing your research and your computer?"

If the professor planned to press charges, someone would need to make long-term arrangements for Rapunzel. As kind as Chief Garris had been in letting the little dog stay at the police station, he could not allow her to do so for long.

Beverly looked thoughtful. "How did she seem to feel about it?"

"She definitely regretted it. She said it was a quick decision and a bad one."

Beverly nodded, a satisfied expression on her face. "Considering how it all turned out, I don't see the need to spread more misery. I'll get ahold of the police and let them know I don't wish to see Deb prosecuted. If they don't think she murdered Vanessa, then I'd rather put the whole thing behind me. Pressing charges is one kind of publicity I would rather not have."

The cat crept along the second-floor corridor. His person had retrieved that disagreeable canine from the kennels earlier this morning, and he wanted to see if the dog was safely back in her own room, where she belonged. The cat didn't even want to consider that his human might welcome the dog into the sanctuary of their cottage.

He'd also found something that his person needed to see.

As he prowled the hallway, the door to one of the rooms opened and a human stepped out.

The cat darted behind a potted plant near the door and peeked through the leaves. But he wasn't fast enough.

The human spotted him and called, "Here, kitty, kitty."

He stayed rooted to the spot. After all, he didn't know this human, and he prided himself on being more cautious than his person, who tended to fling herself headlong into things without thinking them through. He had saved her on many such occasions.

The human opened a small bag, removed a few treats, and held them out.

The cat felt his willpower begin to waver when he recognized the bag and the mouthwatering aroma. They were tunaroons, his favorite treat, made by his person's friend.

The human knelt down and dropped a few pieces on the floor.

How bad could someone who offered tunaroons really be? He trotted over and sniffed the treats, then stopped and glanced up at the person.

The human smiled and petted him. "What a nice kitty. Don't you want a treat?"

His whiskers twitched in anticipation. He knew he should be more guarded, but he was so hungry. He hadn't had anything since his breakfast at home, and that had just been his regular kibble. Nothing nearly as tempting as tunaroons.

Finally giving in, the cat began eating the tasty morsels.

When they were gone, the human picked him up. "My, someone was hungry. Let's go find you some more treats, shall we?"

The day had grown unseasonably warm. The sun shone down brightly, and Faith decided she would like nothing better than to eat her lunch outdoors.

She grabbed the sack lunch that she'd brought from home, then headed for a bench on the grounds where she could admire the sea. It wasn't often this early in the year that the idea of sitting still in the path of an ocean breeze sounded appealing. But the day was mild enough that Faith decided to risk it.

She sat down on the sunny stone bench and soaked up the sunlight while she ate her ham sandwich and an oatmeal and chocolate chip cookie.

As she finished her lunch, a flash of movement caught her attention. Bernadette was walking along the beach.

Bernadette paused and knelt down to inspect something on the shoreline.

Faith headed for the steep staircase that connected the top of the cliff with the beach below. After what had happened to Vanessa, Faith was even more inclined to be careful on the stairs. She held tightly to the handrail, then broke into a jog at the bottom of the staircase to close the gap between them. She reached Bernadette as the younger woman halted at the edge of a tide pool.

"Good afternoon," Bernadette said with a smile. "It's a lovely day for a walk, isn't it?"

"That's just what I thought," Faith said. "I saw you down here, and it inspired me to get some exercise. Do you mind if I join you, or were you interested in a little solitude?"

"I would be glad of some company," Bernadette said as she began walking again.

Faith fell into step next to her.

Bernadette gestured at the beach and the sparkling water beyond. "You must love working here at the manor."

"Working at the library is a dream come true, and I'm extremely fortunate," Faith said. "Your job seems pretty wonderful too. It must feel great to get your books published."

"That's true. I do consider myself to be quite lucky as well. Not as lucky as others, but maybe I'll be able to write full-time someday."

"Beverly was just telling me that she thinks you're a wonderful writer and you deserve to be more recognized," Faith said.

Bernadette stopped and bent down to pick up a razor clamshell. She examined it before slipping it into her pocket. "It's a funny business. There's no clear path to success, and you never know how things will go."

"Would you say there's a significant amount of luck involved?"

Bernadette nodded. "And authors are frequently jealous of successful peers."

"Like Vanessa?" Faith asked. "I imagine many authors wanted to trade places with her."

Bernadette shook her head vigorously. "Vanessa was well-known and made a lot of money from her books, but I wouldn't have traded places with her for anything."

"Why not?" Faith said. "She seemed like she had so much going for her in her writing career."

"I may not be able to live on what I earn from my books," Bernadette responded, "but at least I write what I like."

"Vanessa didn't like the books that she wrote?" Faith asked. "Are you saying she was just writing them for the money?" She had not considered the possibility.

"Are you surprised by that?" Bernadette answered. "After all, Louisa May Alcott only wrote the Little Women books because she needed the money. I expect Vanessa found herself in a similar position."

"So, in a way, Vanessa was a victim of her own success," Faith mused.

"I wouldn't have called her a victim, at least not of success," Bernadette said. "She seemed happy with her fame and fortune."

"You think there was some part of her life she wasn't happy with?" Faith asked.

Bernadette shrugged. "Possibly. I wondered if she even enjoyed her work."

"Why do you say that?" Faith asked.

"I tried to talk writing processes with her once," Bernadette said. "Most authors love talking shop, but she seemed to have very little interest in the nuts and bolts or in the characters whose stories she was continuing. It felt like she couldn't wait to end the conversation or at least change the subject."

"Did she say anything about her writing?"

"She asked me if I had any writing tips to share with her, and it caught me off guard," Bernadette replied. "I told her I would have a hard time telling her anything she didn't already know."

"What did she say?" Faith asked.

"She confided that she was having trouble with writer's block and that it had never happened before," Bernadette said. "She asked me if I had ever experienced it myself and how I had dealt with it."

"Were you able to give her any advice?" Faith asked.

Bernadette shook her head. "That's what I meant about not wanting to trade places with Vanessa. I may not make much money from my writing, but I always find my books so engaging that I can't wait to get to work on them every day."

"I know how you feel," Faith said. "I love most aspects of my job too."

"One thing I wouldn't like is dealing with the pressure that often accompanies publishing success," Bernadette said.

"What sort of pressure?" Faith asked.

"Vanessa was surprisingly frank about her troubles. I think she was feeling completely overwhelmed. She told me that she was desperate because she had missed her deadline, and the publisher was threatening her with legal action if she didn't submit her manuscript soon."

"That sounds serious," Faith said.

"It is," Bernadette agreed. "It doesn't happen very often, and I got the impression that she was panicked about it. She was on the verge of tears when she told me."

"When did you talk to Vanessa about all this?"

"Just before the unveiling ceremony. We left our suites at almost the same time, and we fell into step down the hallway. She told me she had something she wanted to ask me and invited me back to her room after the unveiling."

"She seemed fine at the ceremony," Faith said. "I had no idea she had been upset."

"I was impressed that she managed to pull herself together," Bernadette said. "I'm not sure I would have been able to."

"Is that when she told you about her problems with her publisher?" Faith said.

Bernadette nodded. "I believe Vanessa died an unhappy woman."

Faith wondered about Vanessa's writer's block. "Did Vanessa give any indication which book she had been stuck on?"

"I got the impression she was talking about the first one in the series."

"That's strange. At the ball, her agent announced that she had stockpiled several manuscripts and that the publishing house would be releasing them on time. That doesn't make sense if she was struggling with writer's block, does it?"

"All I can tell you is what Vanessa told me," Bernadette said. "Maybe I misunderstood which book she was struggling with. Perhaps it was several books into the series, and I only assumed it was the first one."

"That could explain it," Faith said. "How did the rest of the conversation go?"

"I found Vanessa rather intimidating, and I wasn't all that eager to keep talking to her, especially with how negative she was about a job I love. As soon as I could, I made up an excuse to leave."

Faith mulled it over. So Bernadette had been in Vanessa's room too. Could she have anything to do with Vanessa's murder or with the theft of *The Damsel's Fate*? Their suites were pretty close, so Bernadette would have been in a position to observe Vanessa coming and going quite easily.

Faith hated to consider that Bernadette might be a suspect in either of the crimes since she seemed like such a sweet young woman. But appearances could be deceiving, and Bernadette had the means and the motive for both the murder and the theft.

Perhaps Bernadette was a very strong suspect indeed.

20

Despite the warmth of the afternoon, Faith had to admit she felt cold after spending so long in the stiff breeze talking to Bernadette. After they parted ways, Faith decided to head back to her cottage to change into a heavier sweater and a jacket.

Even though the manor was warm, there was nothing like slipping into a thick, cuddly sweater to take away the chill, especially when it felt more than skin-deep.

As she opened the door of the cottage and stepped into the tiny foyer, she felt the same pleasure she always experienced when she entered her cozy home. Everything about the space made her heart sing. It had been so carefully and lovingly renovated that it was a joy to simply stand in the middle of the living room and let her gaze wander.

While the wind had picked up outside, the temperature in the cottage was toasty. Coals still glowed in the fireplace grate. A shaft of sunshine streaming through a long window lit up Watson's favorite spot on the back of the couch in the living room.

With a frown, Faith realized she had not seen her cat since they had arrived at work that morning. He was probably still at the manor or spending the day roaming around the grounds outside. If she didn't see him on her walk to the manor, she'd search for him when she got there.

She selected a thick cable-knit sweater from her dresser, tugged it on over her head, and hurried out the door.

Faith did not come across Watson by the time she reached the manor. She wondered if he had taken offense at the fact that he'd been left behind while Rapunzel had accompanied Faith on an errand. She wouldn't be surprised if he was hiding somewhere in an effort to avoid the entire situation, even though Rapunzel was now at the police station with Deb. She'd be sure to give her cat a few tunaroons in apology.

As she made her way through the manor, she found Carol Lynn settled in a wingback chair in one of the reading nooks. Recalling how the fan-fiction writer and Deb had each claimed the other had been the last one to board the bus, Faith decided a conversation was in order.

Carol Lynn glanced up from her book when Faith approached.

"Mind if I join you?" Faith asked.

"Be my guest."

Faith sat in the chair opposite and propped her feet up on the plush ottoman positioned between them. It felt good to rest for a few minutes after her long walk along the beach. She pointed at the copy of *Jo's Boys* in Carol Lynn's hands. "What do you think of it?"

Carol Lynn placed her finger in the book to mark her place. "It's the kind of book that has been saved by Vanessa's most timely death."

"I know you were angry at Vanessa," Faith said, "but that sounds a bit harsh, don't you think?"

"You're right. She didn't deserve to die just because she was a thief." Carol Lynn sighed. "Besides, I was looking forward to having my day in court. Now, I won't have that opportunity."

"A lawsuit can cost a great deal of money," Faith pointed out. "Perhaps it's a good thing that you can no longer pursue it."

"Maybe so," Carol Lynn said. "So has the murder been solved? I heard they arrested Deb."

"Not yet," Faith said. "The police no longer believe that Deb is the only suspect in the murder."

"Who do they suspect?"

"I think they're considering a number of people, particularly ones who had known conflicts with Vanessa," Faith said. "You certainly didn't hide your anger toward her during the panel discussion."

"Of course I was angry. She stole my idea and insulted fan-fiction writers," Carol Lynn said, straightening in her chair. "But I just wanted her to acknowledge that I was the one who came up with the idea for the Littlest Women series. I didn't kill her."

"There also seems to be some question as to where you were the morning of her death," Faith said. She watched for signs of guilt on Carol Lynn's face. Was it her imagination, or did Carol Lynn wince?

"What do you mean?" Carol Lynn demanded. "Has someone been accusing me of something?"

"It was more that your accusation was refuted."

"What accusation?"

"That Deb was the last one to board the bus for the field trip to Orchard House that morning," Faith said.

"It's true," Carol Lynn said. "I watched her sit down in one of the last seats, and then the bus took off."

"But Deb said that you got on the bus after her," Faith responded. "She said that you were the last person to board the bus and she was the second to last."

"Well, she would be looking to blame someone else if she killed Vanessa, wouldn't she?" Carol Lynn argued. "The police seem to think she did it. After all, they arrested her."

"They did," Faith agreed. "But like I said, they're rethinking the possibility of her guilt."

"Are they planning to release her?" Carol Lynn asked. Faith thought she detected a flicker of fear on the other woman's face.

"I expect Deb will be back at the manor before the end of the day," Faith said. "There was simply no way she had enough time between dropping her dog off at the kennels and boarding the bus to murder Vanessa."

Faith didn't mention that Deb had stolen Beverly's research. Since Beverly had decided not to press charges, Faith didn't want to spread that bit of news.

"Guilty or not, Deb is mistaken," Carol Lynn said, her voice becoming shrill. "She was the last one to board the bus."

"Are you sure?" Faith asked innocently. "If you're caught in a lie, it will only make you seem suspicious to the police."

Carol Lynn wrung her hands. "Okay, I lied about Deb being the last one on the bus. It was me but not because I killed Vanessa. You have to believe me," she pleaded. "I would never do something like that."

"If you weren't involved in Vanessa's murder, then why would you cast suspicion on someone else?" Faith asked. "That's not something an innocent person would do."

"I was busy working on something, and I lost track of time," Carol Lynn said. "I promise it had nothing to do with Vanessa's death."

"What were you doing?" Faith asked.

Carol Lynn sat silently for a moment as though weighing her options. Finally, she took a deep breath, then exhaled slowly. "I was working on the second edition of the fake newsletter. The first one aggravated Vanessa so much that I decided to do another one." She sagged against the back of the chair.

"You wrote all those hateful things?" Faith exclaimed. "And after Theresa, Meredith, and Bernadette worked so hard on the real newsletter. How could you?"

"I was just so angry," Carol Lynn said. "I was humiliated by the way Vanessa attacked me in front of the people at the panel. I decided that if she could embarrass me, then I could do the same to her."

Faith considered what Carol Lynn had said. Most people would not be moved to something as extreme as committing murder because they had been publicly humiliated. Taking revenge by coming up with a sensational and unkind newsletter seemed far more reasonable, especially coming from a writer.

Then she remembered some of the things Carol Lynn had written in the newsletter. "How did you know Vanessa was suffering from writer's block and that she was close to missing her deadline?"

"Bernadette told me," Carol Lynn replied.

So it was back to Bernadette. Had she known what Carol Lynn

was up to when she told the fan-fiction writer that bit of gossip? Either way, it was unprofessional of her to share Vanessa's confidence like that.

But for now, Faith was more inclined to believe Carol Lynn's only crime was spreading malicious gossip rather than theft of a rare volume or murder. Still, she really needed some form of proof.

"I appreciate your taking responsibility for the substituted newsletter, but I'm not sure that gets you off the suspect list for the murder," Faith admitted. "Couldn't you have written the newsletter at any time after your confrontation with Vanessa?"

"My computer can prove it," Carol Lynn said. "It always records the time when I save a file. I know I saved the newsletter just before I ran to catch the bus."

Faith stood up. "The police will definitely ask you the same questions I just did. If I were you, I would show them your computer as soon as they arrive to question you." She walked away, glad to have one mystery cleared up.

But she had made no further progress with the other mysteries that remained.

Faith was determined to tackle her ever-increasing to-do list as soon as she stepped through the library door. As much as she enjoyed working with the patrons at the library, she hoped the afternoon would be fairly quiet so she could get her work done.

But a few guests walked in even before she made it to her desk. Fortunately, none of them seemed to need her attention. Two of them headed to the chairs in front of the fireplace, and the other patron proceeded to the biography section.

When the guests were occupied, Faith continued to her desk and sat down. As she reached for a pad of paper and a pen to put her thoughts in order, she noticed an envelope propped up against her pencil cup.

Her name was written across the front in block letters. She didn't recognize the handwriting. While it wasn't unusual for guests or even for staff at the manor to leave notes for her on her desk, there was something strange about the appearance of the letter.

She lifted the flap on the envelope, noting that it had not been sealed but rather simply tucked inside. She withdrew a piece of Castleton Manor stationery, the kind found in all the guest rooms and the office center.

The note was written in the same plain style and with a felt-tip pen, but the message made Faith's blood run cold.

I have taken Watson. If you ever want to see your cat again, you will leave Castleton Manor's copy of The Maiden's Plight *on the piano in the music room at 5 p.m. sharp.*

Don't call the police, or you'll regret it.

21

Faith's heart hammered in her chest. Someone had taken Watson and was holding him for ransom. How could this be happening? For a moment, she couldn't even move.

Then she reached for the phone on her desk and called Wolfe.

He picked up on the third ring. "Good afternoon. What a pleasant surprise."

"Could you please come to the library?" she blurted, fighting back tears.

"I'll be right down," Wolfe said without hesitation.

She remained in her chair, trying to remember to breathe as she waited for what seemed like an eternity for him to arrive.

Just as she wondered if she should call him again, he rushed through the door of the library. "What's wrong?"

Faith burst into tears.

The few patrons in the library turned to see what the commotion was about.

Wolfe went over to the guests. "I'm so sorry, but we need to close the library for a little while. I appreciate your understanding." He escorted them to the door and locked it behind them, then hurried back to Faith. "What's happened?"

"I found this on my desk," she said, handing him the ransom note.

As Wolfe read the note, his eyes widened. "You didn't see who left it?"

Faith shook her head. "None of the patrons were behaving suspiciously," she said, her voice trembling. "I can't believe anyone would take Watson."

"It must be the same person who stole Vanessa's copy of *The*

Damsel's Fate," Wolfe said. "The book will be even more valuable if the thief can pair it with *The Maiden's Plight*."

"It's horrible to think Watson was snatched because of a book," Faith said.

"The person who took him realizes that you are in a position of trust and that you might be able to be pressured into stealing it if you believed Watson was in danger," Wolfe said. "It was really very clever of them."

Faith felt her eyes filling with tears once more.

"I'm so sorry. That's not what you need to be thinking about right now. You must be in an absolute panic." Wolfe handed Faith a neatly pressed linen handkerchief.

"Thank you," she said as she dabbed tears from her eyes. "I have absolutely no idea what to do."

"It's obvious to me what has to be done," Wolfe said.

"You don't think we should call the police, do you?" Faith asked. "What will happen to Watson if we do?"

"No, we won't involve the police just yet. I don't want to risk it," Wolfe said. "But I think we'll be able to get Watson back and discover who stole Vanessa's copy of *The Damsel's Fate* at the same time. Perhaps we'll even be able to unmask her killer too."

"What makes you so sure we'll be able to do all that without the police?" Faith asked, though a flicker of hope sparked in her heart because Wolfe seemed so confident.

"We have a decided advantage that I am sure the culprit is not aware of," Wolfe answered. "Otherwise, the person never would have chosen the music room as the drop-off point for the ransom." He smiled. "I'm certain we'll get Watson back safe and sound before the evening is over."

The hair on the back of Faith's neck stood up as she entered the music room and placed Castleton Manor's copy of *The Maiden's Plight* on the piano as the ransom note had instructed. While she had every hope that Wolfe's plan would succeed, she still felt her stomach tied in knots.

Where was Watson now? Was whoever had taken him being kind to him? It was all she could do to keep from bursting into tears as she turned from the piano and walked out of the room.

Faith passed many of the retreat attendees in the hallway. She scanned their faces, wondering if one of them was guilty of stealing her beloved cat. She was not a suspicious person by nature, and she was surprised at how strange it felt to wonder if everyone she encountered could have done such a terrible thing.

She followed Wolfe's suggestion and meandered throughout the manor, so that whoever had taken Watson would know she was nowhere near the music room. When she was sure she was not being observed, she slipped down the stairs that led to the wine cellar. She made her way to the back wall, grasped the hidden latch on it, and swung open the door cleverly disguised by shelves holding bottle after bottle of the manor's extensive wine collection.

After shutting the door behind her, Faith hurried along the secret passage, eager to reach Wolfe before the ransom was collected. She was grateful that while the passageway had plenty of twists, there were no other tunnels leading off the main corridor.

Eventually she climbed a set of stairs to meet Wolfe at the top.

He turned to her and held a finger to his lips.

She nodded and joined him.

Wolfe pointed at two small openings built into the wall in front of them.

Faith realized they were peeking out through tiny gaps in the decorative plaster built into the back wall of the music room. She pressed her face against the opening in the wall. Sure enough, she was able to see clearly into the music room. Her gaze took in the room inspired by the finest French buildings with its furniture upholstered in velvet. The book on top of the piano was in plain sight.

As theatrical as the room's decor was, it had never felt as dramatic as it did in that moment as she peered at it through the narrow opening, praying for Watson's safe return.

After what felt like ages, the door to the music room slowly opened.

Faith held her breath.

Theresa Collins stepped into the room.

22

Faith almost gasped. She didn't know who she had expected to walk through the door of the music room to collect the ransom for Watson, but it definitely hadn't been the president of the Pickwick Club.

Faith liked Theresa, and she had enjoyed working on the newsletter with her. She couldn't believe that the woman had done something like this. Was it possible that Theresa had simply decided she wanted to explore the music room with no nefarious purpose in mind?

Theresa glanced around the room before pulling a pair of white gloves from the bag slung over her shoulder. She put on the gloves and advanced to the piano, then picked up the copy of *The Maiden's Plight* and slid it carefully into her bag.

That answers that question, Faith thought sadly.

When Theresa started toward the door, Faith grabbed Wolfe's arm.

He pressed firmly on a latch in the wall of the alcove, and the hidden door swung out silently. "I'm afraid it's not going to be that easy," Wolfe said firmly. "If you don't want me to call the police, I suggest you tell us where Watson is at once."

Theresa spun around at the sound of his voice. Faith thought she had never seen anyone appear so startled in her life. All the color drained from her face, and she was visibly trembling.

Faith still didn't want to believe that Theresa was capable of this. Maybe she was simply collecting the ransom for the real thief.

"I promise Watson is fine," Theresa said, dashing Faith's hopes. "I would never hurt him."

Wolfe crossed the room in a few long strides and held out his hand.

Theresa slipped the bag from her shoulder, removed the book, and passed it to him.

"What have you done with Watson?" Faith said as she rushed to Theresa's side.

"He's in the bathroom in my suite," Theresa answered. "Don't worry. He's fine. I've taken good care of him."

"Did you steal Vanessa's copy of *The Damsel's Fate*?" Wolfe asked. Theresa nodded.

"Why did you do it?" Faith asked. "And then you made it worse by taking Watson. How could you?" She heard the anger in her own voice and felt tears pricking behind her eyes.

"The cost of the retreat had spiraled out of control," Theresa explained. "I miscalculated the costs for the attendees, and fewer people signed up than I expected. Then Vanessa's demands for a higher fee because of the pets on-site pushed the whole thing into the red. It would have been unprofessional to ask those who had already signed up to pay more, and I didn't have enough money to come up with the difference."

"Why didn't you talk to us?" Wolfe asked gently. "We could have come up with a solution together."

Theresa hung her head. "I didn't want you to think I didn't know what I was doing. It never occurred to me that you'd be so accommodating."

"Did you kill Vanessa to get her book?" Faith demanded. Maybe Wolfe was feeling understanding, but this woman had taken and threatened Watson, so Faith wasn't ready to let her off the hook just yet.

Theresa looked stricken. "Of course not. Why would you think I would do such a terrible thing?"

"I wouldn't have before you took Watson and threatened to never let me see him again," Faith said sharply. "I wouldn't put anything past you at this point."

Theresa's face crumpled. "I swear I didn't kill Vanessa. The night before she died, she invited me into her suite, only to berate me about Deb Fremont attending the conference. I reminded her that she hadn't asked for a list of attendees before the event began."

"That sounds very unreasonable of her," Wolfe said. "But how does that lead to you stealing her copy of *The Damsel's Fate*?"

Theresa took a deep breath. "While I was in her suite, she went into the bathroom. She had left the book sitting on a side table, and I realized I could sell it and make back the money I had to take out of my own pocket for the conference. I was angry and stressed and not thinking clearly. So I slid it into my bag and left."

"Even if what you say is true, the police are going to have a lot of questions for you," Wolfe said. "The theft of Vanessa's book sounds like a really good motive. If you killed her, she couldn't accuse you of stealing it from her room."

Something was tickling at Faith's memory. Even though she was so furious with Theresa that she was having trouble breathing, she realized she could provide her with an alibi for the time of the murder.

"Actually, Theresa didn't do it," Faith said. "As the conference organizer, she had to be at the bus first. She wouldn't have had time that morning to commit the murder."

"That's right," Theresa said, relief in her voice. "You can check with the bus driver about the time I arrived. And plenty of people saw me in the breakfast room before I left for the bus."

"I'll be sure to tell the police so they can verify your alibi," Wolfe said. "If Watson is safe and you return Vanessa's copy of *The Damsel's Fate*, you may be able to avoid jail time."

"I'll take you to Watson right away," Theresa said. "I can give you back Vanessa's copy of the book, too, while we're there. I've been keeping it in my room."

"Let's go," Wolfe urged.

Faith and Wolfe followed Theresa out of the music room and upstairs.

Theresa turned the key in the lock of her suite and opened the door.

Faith immediately noticed that Theresa had left the clock radio in the room tuned to a classical music station. She must have wanted to drown out any sound that Watson might have made.

Faith rushed ahead of Theresa and ran to open the door of the opulent bathroom at the far end of the suite.

There, sitting on a tufted vanity chair, was Watson. He blinked at her as if to ask, "What's the big idea? I'm relaxing."

Faith cried in relief as she scooped her cat into her arms.

Watson snuggled against her chest and purred.

"Oh, Rumpy, I've been so worried about you," Faith said. "How did Theresa manage to lure you in here?"

She couldn't imagine Watson being easily tricked. Generally, he had exceptional judgment when it came to people. Faith found it very surprising that he would have attached himself to someone unsavory.

She scanned the bathroom for clues that would explain how Theresa had convinced him to follow her into her suite.

Watson gave one last lingering purr before jumping from her arms and landing lightly on the floor. He went to the wastepaper basket near the sink and sat down. He meowed and patted the basket with one paw.

Faith walked over and peered into the trash can. She spotted a familiar bag from Happy Tails inside. "That explains it," she said, removing the bag. She opened it and peeked inside. Sure enough, there were still a few crumbs of tunaroons.

"I always knew your stomach would get you into trouble one day," Faith said. She returned the bag to the trash, then picked Watson up and left the bathroom.

Theresa was handing Vanessa's copy of *The Damsel's Fate* to Wolfe.

"See, I told you he was all right," Theresa said, motioning to Watson. "I really didn't intend to cause any harm. I was just desperate."

"Desperate or not, the police will need to be told what happened here," Wolfe said.

"Now that you've gotten Watson and the book back, do you really need to tell them?" Theresa pleaded. "It's the first time I've ever done anything like this in my life."

Wolfe glanced at Faith and arched an eyebrow at her as if to ask for her opinion.

Faith clutched Watson more firmly to her chest. As much as she hated to act hard-hearted, especially since Watson seemed no worse for the wear, she knew that Chief Garris would need to be informed, if only to eliminate Theresa from his suspect list for the murder. She nodded ever so slightly.

Wolfe faced Theresa. "I'm sorry, but it's out of our hands."

"Even though we recovered the book, the police were already alerted to the theft," Faith said. "They'll have to be told that it's been returned, and they'll want to know how and by whom. They'll also need to know about your alibi for the time of the murder."

"The sooner we let them know, the easier it will be for you," Wolfe told Theresa. "The chief is a very understanding man. If you really had nothing to do with Vanessa's murder, they may let the whole matter drop."

"Do you really think so?" Theresa asked, her voice quavering with worry.

"If your alibi for the murder checks out, I'll put in a good word for you with the chief," Wolfe said. "I'll let him know that you returned the book of your own volition and that it wasn't damaged."

"What about taking Watson?" Theresa said, turning to Faith.

Faith scratched her cat's ears. "We won't mention what happened to the police as long as you promise never to do something like that again."

"Of course not. I don't know how to thank you enough," Theresa said, bursting into tears.

"Maybe you should volunteer at a local animal shelter in an effort to make up for what you've done," Faith suggested.

Watson jumped from Faith's arms and trotted over to Theresa. He rested one paw on her pant leg and stood there as she bent down to pet him.

Faith shook her head. Her cat never failed to surprise her.

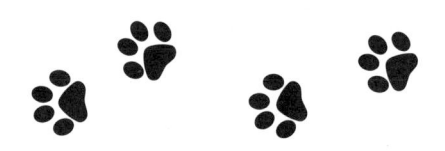

The cat didn't understand what all the fuss was about. He thought his human was almost too glad to see him as she picked him up once more.

Although he was usually delighted by her attention, there was something he had meant to show her before he had been distracted by that bag of tunaroons. There was no more time to waste.

As they left the room, he leaped from his human's arms and landed a few feet ahead of her in the corridor. The cat ran ahead, certain she would not let him out of her sight for long, not after the way she had cried when she found him locked so unceremoniously in a bathroom. He raced for the stairs and paused halfway down, glancing back over his shoulder to make sure she was following him.

When she caught up, he darted for the hallway. He paused to see if she was still behind him, then ducked inside the office center and pounced onto the largest metal machine in the room.

"What are you doing up there?" his human asked. "Marlene will have a fit if she finds out you've been sitting on the new photocopier." She reached out to pick him up.

He arched his back.

"What's gotten into you?" she asked as she lifted him from the machine. She placed him on the floor and stared down at him.

He loved her dearly, but sometimes she was so obtuse. The cat stood up on his hind legs and tapped the front of the machine.

"What is it, Rumpy?" his human asked.

He let out a loud series of meows, attempting to make her understand while scolding her for the use of the horrible nickname.

"Okay, I'll check it out." She lifted the top of the machine.

The cat nudged her leg with his nose. She was getting warmer, but he'd shown her exactly where to look.

She closed the top. "There's nothing here."

He let out a howl and batted the front of the copier with his paw again.

His human finally seemed to understand. She crouched and opened the machine, then peered inside. "Is it the paper?"

He bumped her leg again.

She studied the lights blinking on the front of the machine. "There's a paper jam. Is that what you wanted me to see?"

The cat began to purr as loudly as he could. There was no way she could fail to understand him now.

His person reached into the back of the mechanism and, after a short struggle, pulled out a crumpled piece of paper. She closed the machine and placed the paper on top of it.

He watched with satisfaction as she smoothed out the paper and read the words printed on the smudged page.

"Watson, you've lived up to your name once again," his human announced. "I think you've solved Vanessa's murder."

23

Faith took the piece of paper and rushed out of the office center with Watson at her heels.

As they hurried down the corridor, they saw Marlene.

"Have you seen Meredith Harris or Marcus Tripp this evening?" Faith asked her.

"Chief Garris just asked me the same thing," Marlene answered, raising an eyebrow.

"Did he say why he wanted them?"

"He said that you and Wolfe had recovered Vanessa's book and he wanted to return it to Vanessa's estate," Marlene replied. "He thought one of them would know how to do that."

"Where did you send him?" Faith said. She felt her impatience rising. "It's really quite important."

Marlene crossed her arms over her chest. "I'll tell you the same thing I told him. While I am not tasked with the responsibility of knowing where all our guests are at any given time, I believe I saw the two of them heading for the billiard room."

Faith didn't wait for Marlene to ask her any questions. She and Watson rushed off to the billiard room.

As she entered the room, she considered it strange that such a luxurious space built for fun and games was where the solution to such a grisly crime would be announced.

Chief Garris stood at the head of the billiard table examining Vanessa's copy of *The Damsel's Fate*. Marcus and Meredith held cues and were taking turns at the table. Marcus's dog, Maisie, sat in one of the chairs at a small table nestled along the side of the room.

Meredith turned to Faith. "I hear we have you to thank for the good news about the recovery of *The Damsel's Fate*."

"I'm glad it was found undamaged," Faith said. "But that's not the most interesting book-related news I've discovered today."

Marcus sank a shot in the right corner pocket, then straightened up and gave Faith his full attention.

"What did you learn?" the chief prompted.

She took a step toward him and held out the piece of paper from the photocopier.

"What's this?" Garris asked.

"I believe it's proof of who actually had the best reason to murder Vanessa," Faith said. "Meredith, can you explain this?" She pointed to the paper in the chief's hand.

"Since I don't know what it is, I would be hard-pressed to explain it," Meredith said coolly, but Faith thought she saw a flicker of fear pass over the assistant's attractive features.

Marcus's face appeared flushed. Even Maisie seemed slightly uncomfortable as she shifted in the chair.

"Where did you find it?" the chief asked.

"It was jammed in the photocopier in the office center," Faith said. "I believe it belongs to you, Meredith."

"That still doesn't explain what it is," Meredith said, moving toward the chief and holding out her hand.

Garris ignored her and scanned the paper. "It looks like a page from a contract between you and the publisher for Ms. Langston's Littlest Women series," he said. "It seems to be offering a contract for the same series to you instead."

"Marcus announced at the ball that Vanessa had written several of the books in the series before she died and that the publishing house planned to release them on schedule," Faith said. "If that were true, why would they need a contract with you, Meredith?"

Meredith lifted her chin and glared at them defiantly.

"This has nothing to do with me," Marcus said hastily. "This is between you and Meredith." He returned his billiard cue to the rack on the wall and made as if to scoop Maisie from the chair.

"Not so fast, Mr. Tripp," the chief said. "Since you're listed as the agent handling the contract, it has a great deal to do with you."

Marcus's face turned an even brighter shade of red. Maisie began to whine, and he reached down and scratched her ears. He glanced over at Meredith and then at Faith. "Meredith said it was an accident," he blurted out. "It seemed like divine intervention when Vanessa fell down the stairs. I had nothing to do with the murder. I didn't know any better."

"That's not entirely true," Faith argued. "After the police began the investigation, everyone knew that Vanessa had been murdered."

"Even if Miss Harris had told you that it was an accident, you should have come to us right away," Garris said.

"But I had no part in harming Vanessa," Marcus protested.

"At the very least you are an accessory after the fact," the chief told him. "If you tell me what you know, we may be able to cut you a deal with the prosecution."

"You coward! You promised you wouldn't blab!" Meredith raised her billiard cue over her head as if to strike Marcus with it.

Garris stepped forward and wrenched it from her hands. "That's enough. Now take a seat over there away from the door while Mr. Tripp explains what happened. It seems like he's far more interested in cooperating than you are."

Meredith's shoulders slumped in defeat. She sank into the chair opposite Maisie and drew her knees up to her chest, wrapping her arms around them and hugging them tightly to her chest.

"Did all of this start because Vanessa developed writer's block?" Faith asked.

"No, not really," Marcus said. He sighed. "It had far more to do with the fact that Vanessa never wrote anything in the first place."

"What do you mean?" Faith asked.

"Meredith wrote all of Vanessa's books," Marcus admitted. "All but the Littlest Women series."

Faith's eyes widened in astonishment, and she whirled around to stare at the assistant. "You wrote all of Vanessa's books?"

Meredith somehow managed to make herself look even smaller as she squeezed herself into a tinier ball.

"I don't understand. Wasn't Ms. Langston a best-selling author?" Garris tucked the crumpled copy of the contract into his pocket and began scribbling in his notepad.

Marcus shook his head. "Vanessa was great at being famous. She had a flair for the dramatic, a very photogenic face, and a theatrical style that went over well at public appearances. What she didn't have was actual writing ability. That was where Meredith came in."

"But why wouldn't you want to take credit for writing the books?" Faith asked Meredith.

"I hated the idea of the spotlight," Meredith said. "I'm very introverted, and I prefer to remain in the background."

Faith could understand her reluctance, but it was still a shock. After all, Bernadette was also an introvert, but she didn't have a ghostwriter. On the other hand, she hadn't been quite as big as Vanessa—or, rather, Meredith. "How did that work?"

"Vanessa and I had an agreement," Meredith explained. "I accompanied her as her assistant, but I actually spent most of my time writing the books. She got the attention she craved, and we split the paycheck."

"It seems like it was an arrangement that suited both of you," Faith said. "So what went wrong?"

"It worked well until Vanessa came up with the idea to write the Littlest Women series," Marcus chimed in. "After spending so much time pretending to be a writer, she suddenly believed she really was one."

"More importantly, she was tired of splitting the proceeds," Meredith added. "She took the idea for the series to the publisher without mentioning it to Marcus or me."

"Did the publishing house know that you had written her other books?" Faith asked.

"Not until after her death," Meredith said. "When Marcus told them the truth, they offered me a contract to continue the series. We agreed to keep Vanessa's name on the covers because it would help them to sell well."

The chief glanced up from his notes. "I expect the publicity surrounding Ms. Langston's death made her name all the more valuable."

"Did you make the announcement at the ball because Meredith had gotten the contract with the publishing house to take over for Vanessa?" Faith said.

"Yes. Publishing is a tough business, and you have to make the most of every opportunity," Marcus said. "It seemed like a great place to build buzz for the books despite Vanessa's passing."

"I think you mean her murder," Garris corrected sharply.

"Like I said before, Meredith told me it was an accident," Marcus insisted, then faced Meredith. "Tell them I didn't know anything about it."

Meredith leaned back in the chair and shut her eyes.

"What exactly happened?" the chief asked.

"The publisher rejected Vanessa's manuscript," Meredith answered. "They said the caliber of her work was completely unacceptable and that if she didn't fix it fast, they would cancel her contract."

"When Meredith filled me in, I tried to talk to Vanessa about it," Marcus said. "I suggested that Meredith could take over the new series, but she wouldn't hear of it. She said she had decided to find somebody else to ghostwrite the new series for her."

"Vanessa was furious that I told Marcus about the rejection," Meredith remarked. "She said if that was the way I was going to abuse her trust, then she didn't want me writing her other books either."

"So why kill her?" Faith asked. "Why not just out her as the fraud she was and let her sink?"

"Even if Marcus backed up my story, it would have taken money and time in court to prove that I wrote all her books and get credit for them," Meredith said. "Then where would I be? Who among Vanessa's loyal fans would want to read the work of the woman who discredited her and revealed her as a liar?"

"Where are you now?" the chief asked. "You'd have to start from scratch writing under your own name, and Vanessa's not around for you to write under hers."

"We were going to release new books claiming they were manuscripts cowritten between Vanessa and me before her death, and I had finished them," Meredith replied. "We'd eventually release books under my name and hope that her fan base would come over to my books, since they'd be the closest to new Vanessa books anyone would be able to get."

Faith wondered if the scheme would have really worked.

"So you strung the fishing line across the stairs?" Garris asked Meredith.

Meredith nodded. "I knew Vanessa was meeting with Marcus the morning of the field trip and she was always late for appointments. When I mentioned that she was about to be late, she said I should have reminded her earlier and my incompetence was one more reason why she was firing me."

"Then you framed Ms. Fremont by putting a length of fishing line in her purse," the chief continued.

"After I heard that Deb was taken in for questioning, I finagled my way inside her room," Meredith admitted. "While it was being cleaned, I claimed I'd loaned Deb a book and wanted it back since we didn't know if or when she'd be released. Then I slipped the fishing line into her purse."

As Faith thought about Meredith sneaking into Deb's room, she remembered the person skulking in the hallway outside Vanessa's suite. "Were you watching the assistant manager and me when we searched Vanessa's room for her book?"

Meredith nodded. "I'd already looked for it, and I was wondering if I'd missed it somehow."

"How did you know Vanessa would use the back stairs?" Faith asked.

"I told her using them would save her a couple of minutes," Meredith said. "Then I called Marcus and told him Vanessa had decided not to meet with him."

"After you called me, I decided to go for a drive in the country," Marcus said.

"Can you prove that?" the chief asked.

"Yes, but it may add to my problems," Marcus said.

"I doubt it will be worse than murder," Garris said.

"While I was driving, I received a frantic call from another author I represent," Marcus said. "She was having huge issues with her publisher. I was upset about the situation, and I began driving too fast. I didn't see a cyclist on the side of the road until I was right next to her."

"You're the one who ran Bernadette off the road?" Faith asked.

"I feel awful." Marcus hung his head. "I was so relieved that she suffered only minor injuries."

"You're very lucky she wasn't badly hurt. But I can still charge you with a hit-and-run accident. You should have stopped immediately to check on her," Garris said sternly, then focused on Meredith once more. "What happened after you canceled Ms. Langston's meeting with Mr. Tripp?"

"I waited in my room until your officers came to let me know what had happened. It was easy to pretend to be shocked. I think I actually was startled by what I had done and the fact that it had worked. Even now, I still can't quite believe it."

"I think it's going to feel very real, very soon," the chief said. "Meredith Harris and Marcus Tripp, I am arresting you both for the murder of Vanessa Langston."

24

Even though Wolfe had encouraged her to take the day off, Faith did not want to miss the chance to say goodbye to all her fellow Louisa May Alcott fans.

She woke at her regular time and headed over to the manor with Watson, who stayed close to her side rather than wandering on ahead as he usually did.

Faith was sure most of the guests would want to take a last, lingering look at the library. What booklover could resist a final few moments in such a beautiful space?

Another draw to the library was seeing *The Damsel's Fate* and *The Maiden's Plight* displayed together once more. As soon as Vanessa's book had been recovered, Wolfe had locked it in the glass case next to its companion volume until it could be returned to Vanessa's estate.

Shortly after Faith and Watson settled into the library, Beverly entered. She waved to Faith but made a beeline for the display case to study the Alcott books.

"They really are lovely, aren't they?" Faith said as she joined her.

"After all the difficulties that plagued the conference, it's such a joy to see these volumes together again," Beverly said.

"I'm happy you have the chance to see them. I know what it means to you," Faith said. As she reflected on the tragic events, she was reminded of something. "If you don't mind my asking, why were you in Vanessa's room the morning she died?"

"I accused Vanessa of stealing my research, and she denied it," Beverly said. "But I couldn't let it go, so I marched up to her suite. That was when she offered to loan me *The Damsel's Fate* as a sign of good faith. She planned to give it to me before the retreat was over."

Faith nodded.

"What will happen to Vanessa's book?" Beverly asked.

"We're taking care of it while Vanessa's estate is being settled," Faith said. "There's a chance the volumes might remain here together. Mr. Jaxon wishes to purchase Vanessa's copy for the Castleton collection."

"That would be wonderful," Beverly said. "It would be such a shame to separate the books."

"You'll have to come back and visit sometime," Faith said.

"I'd love to, but I doubt I'll be able to visit anytime soon," the professor said with a smile.

"I suppose you'll be hard at work finishing your book now that your research has been returned," Faith said.

"Amongst other things," Beverly said. "I've actually been awarded another contract."

"Congratulations! What's the topic?"

"It's a true crime story giving a behind-the-scenes exposé on Vanessa's murder and the theft of *The Damsel's Fate*," Beverly said. "This time I'm sure I'm writing a best seller."

"I wouldn't be surprised. And if you ever need a quiet place to escape and focus on your writing, we'd be glad to see you again," Faith said.

"After this week, I have trouble imagining that this place is ever quiet, but maybe I'll give it a try."

Deb tentatively walked into the library later that morning. She and Rapunzel both wore subdued beige sweaters that matched their expressions.

Faith got up from her desk and approached her. "Good morning."

Deb glanced around the room. "Is Watson here?"

Faith turned just in time to spot the tip of Watson's bobbed tail as he scurried out of sight. "I'm afraid you just missed him."

Rapunzel leaned in the direction he had gone, but the little dog didn't seem inclined to make a fuss.

"I wanted to thank you both for your kindness during our stay," Deb said. "I don't know what we would have done if you hadn't taken care of Rapunzel. And me for that matter."

"It was no trouble at all," Faith said. "I'm just glad everything worked out in the end." She could feel Watson's judgmental gaze as she gave Rapunzel a final pat before saying goodbye to Deb.

At this point, she was pretty sure she owed the cat his weight in tunaroons.

Bernadette arrived not long after Deb left. Faith was pleased to see the young woman had a spring in her step and a confident set to her shoulders.

"I wanted to be sure to share my good news before I left," Bernadette said with a grin.

"I always love to hear good news," Faith said. "What is it?"

"Vanessa's publisher heard about what happened with Meredith, and they found out I was a panelist here at the conference for my work in this genre," Bernadette said, her eyes shining. "They offered me a contract to write the Littlest Women series!"

"That's wonderful. I can't think of anyone who deserves it more," Faith said honestly. "I think they're lucky to have you for the project."

"Now I just need an agent," Bernadette commented. "But not Marcus, of course. I'd never hire someone who would leave me injured on the side of the road."

"Even if you had wanted to hire him, I don't think he'll be available for a long time," Faith said. "He's being charged as an accessory after the fact in Vanessa's murder. But I'm sure you won't have any trouble landing a good agent."

"I hope you're right."

Faith smiled. "I'll definitely suggest your series to my book club as soon as it's available."

"Thank you." Bernadette gave her a quick hug and headed out the door.

Carol Lynn dropped by with Ferdinand perched jauntily on her shoulder.

"Hello!" the parrot squawked.

Faith was surprised to see Carol Lynn with Meredith's bird. "Is there something I can help you with?"

"We just wanted to visit this magnificent library one last time before we left, didn't we?" Carol Lynn said, stroking the bird's chest with a finger.

He nuzzled her hair with his beak.

Faith smiled. "It looks like you've made a friend."

"When I heard about Meredith, I offered to take care of her parrot," Carol Lynn said. "It's not like he made her kill Vanessa, so I didn't think he should face homelessness."

"That is very kind of you, especially considering that Meredith was going to take over the Littlest Women series," Faith said.

"I must admit that I was angry when I heard about that," Carol Lynn said. "I even wondered if I should file a lawsuit against Meredith for using the idea. But my lawyer urged me to reconsider. He said it would be very difficult and expensive to prove the idea was actually stolen from me."

"That sounds like good advice," Faith said. "Do you have another story in the works?"

Carol Lynn grinned. "As a matter of fact, I do. I'm going to write a children's book about an orphaned parrot. I think it will have a very happy ending. Won't it, Ferdinand?"

"Pretty bird!" the parrot squawked.

As Faith watched the two leave, she thought the story was likely to have a happy ending indeed.

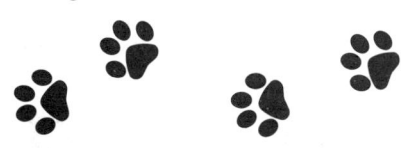

Theresa was the last member of the Pickwick Club to stop in for a final visit to the library.

Faith noticed her hovering in the doorway. She thought Theresa seemed unsure about entering.

Reminding herself that she was a professional, Faith smiled and approached the other woman. "Please come in."

When Theresa stepped across the threshold timidly, Faith was surprised to see she was not alone. She cradled Maisie in her arms.

"I wanted to say goodbye and thank you for all the help you gave me with the conference," Theresa said. "I also wanted to apologize again for any pain I caused you and Watson. I should have considered my actions."

"We all do things we regret from time to time," Faith said, then thought of something. "So, how did you get into the library to leave the ransom note?"

Theresa stared at the floor. "I went to the front desk and said I didn't know where you were and I needed to check a certain book right away. The clerk let me in, and I left the note when she wasn't looking. I'm sorry."

Watson sauntered to Theresa's side. He rubbed against her ankles and then turned his attention to her companion.

"I wanted to let you both know I plan to keep my word about helping out in a local animal shelter when I get home," Theresa said. "But I wanted to do something more. When I heard about Marcus, I offered to take care of Maisie until he's able to be with her again."

As Faith reached over and scratched Maisie behind the ears, she realized that Watson had been right to trust Theresa despite her ransom attempt. After all, better people than Theresa had made horrible decisions in desperation.

"That is very generous of you," Faith said. "I think I can speak for Watson as well as myself when I say all is forgiven."

That evening, Faith and Watson had finally settled in under her grandmother's quilt on the sofa in the gardener's cottage. A fire burned in the grate, and a cheerful glow spread around the snug room. Faith couldn't remember a time when she had felt quite so content to be curled up with her cat and a good book.

Her peace was shattered by a knock on the door.

Faith was tempted to pretend she wasn't home.

But Watson nudged her arm.

"Oh, all right," she grumbled as she pushed back the warm blanket, set her book aside, and got to her feet.

When she opened the heavy wooden door, she saw Wolfe standing bathed in the light from a carriage lantern that was mounted on the front of the cottage. Suddenly she was glad she'd answered the door. Her cat was never wrong.

"Good evening," Wolfe said. "I hope I'm not disturbing you."

"Of course not." Faith stepped back and opened the door wider. "Won't you come in?"

"Thank you." Wolfe took off his coat and hung it on a peg in the foyer, then followed her into the living room.

Faith felt slightly self-conscious as she noticed her coat and shoes haphazardly tossed on the floor. She had simply discarded them where she stood in her haste to collapse on the sofa. If she had known he was coming, she would have tidied up.

"This certainly looks cozy," Wolfe said. "I love spending a cool night by the fire with a good book too. I really hope I haven't interrupted your plans." He paused by the sofa and studied the copy of *Sense and Sensibility* that Faith had set aside when she answered the door.

Watson leaped to the floor and began twining around Wolfe's ankles.

Faith smiled. "As you can see, Watson is very pleased to see you. What can we do for you?"

Wolfe bent down to scratch Watson behind the ears. "I wanted to be sure that you and Watson were all right."

Watson meowed as if in response.

They both laughed.

"I think he means, 'We're fine,'" Faith said. "It was very thoughtful of you to check on us."

"I also wanted to tell you how much I appreciate your help in getting to the bottom of what happened to Vanessa," Wolfe said. "Without your efforts to solve the murder and the theft, the manor's reputation might have been damaged."

Faith felt her cheeks growing slightly flushed at the compliment. To hide her blush, she turned and folded the quilt in half and draped it over the arm of the sofa.

"I really should be thanking you." Faith sat on the couch and motioned for Wolfe to join her.

"I can't imagine why," Wolfe said as he settled beside her.

"It's not everyone who would have been willing to sacrifice such a valuable book from his collection in order to ransom a cat," Faith said.

"It didn't feel like a sacrifice at the time, and it doesn't now."

Faith's pulse began to race. "What do you mean?"

"There is nothing that brings me more joy than doing the things that ensure your happiness," Wolfe said, taking her hand in his large, warm one.

Of all the words he could have said to her, she didn't think any could have surprised her as much as those. Brooke would never let her hear the end of it, but suddenly she didn't mind. She squeezed his hand and beamed at him. "I feel the same way."

The firelight cast a warm glow over Wolfe's handsome features as he smiled back, then leaned forward and gently kissed her.

Her head felt light as she realized how right it felt to be here like this with him.

He pulled away and gazed into her eyes.

Watson jumped up onto the back of the couch and purred.

Wolfe laughed. "Does that mean he approves?"

The cat butted his face against Wolfe's.

Faith smiled. "I know he does."

Wolfe laughed and kissed her once more.

YOUR FEEDBACK MEANS A LOT TO US!

Up to this point, we've been doing all the writing. Now it's *your* turn!

Tell us what you think about this book, the characters, the bad guy, or anything else you'd like to share with us about this series. We can't wait to hear from *you*!

Log on to give us your feedback at:
https://www.surveymonkey.com/r/CastletonLibrary

Annie's FICTION